Mostly Ghostly

Who Let the Ghosts Out?

Experience all the chills of the Mostly Ghostly series!

Mostly Ghostly #1: *Who Let the Ghosts Out?*
Mostly Ghostly #2: *Have You Met My Ghoulfriend?*

AND COMING SOON:

Mostly Ghostly #3: *One Night in Doom House*
Mostly Ghostly #4: *Little Camp of Horrors*

R.L. STINE

DELACORTE PRESS
A PARACHUTE PRESS BOOK

Published by
Delacorte Press
an imprint of
Random House Children's Books
a division of Random House, Inc.
New York

Visit us on the Web! www.randomhouse.com/kids
Educators and librarians, for a variety of teaching tools, visit us at
www.randomhouse.com/teachers

Library of Congress Cataloging-in-Publication Data
Stine, R.L.
Who let the ghosts out? / R.L. Stine.
p. cm.—(Mostly ghostly)
Summary: A boy suddenly finds himself haunted by the friendly ghosts of two children while being pursued by an evil being.
ISBN 0-385-74663-6 (hardcover)—ISBN 0-385-90913-6 (lib. bdg.)
[1. Ghosts—Fiction. 2. Horror stories.] I. Title.
PZ7.S86037Wh 2004
[Fic]—dc22
2003026133

Printed in the United States of America

August 2004

10 9 8 7 6 5 4 3 2 1

BVG

For my nephew, Cody

Here's a new one. . . .

1

MY SISTER AND I were walking home on the night all the horror began.

Clouds floated across the moon. We ducked our heads as a cold wind whipped our cheeks. Above us, the bare tree limbs rattled like skeleton bones.

Shivering, I hugged myself to keep warm. I was wearing a T-shirt and shorts. Why didn't I have my coat?

I turned to my sister. She was shivering too, in a sleeveless T-shirt and low-riding jeans. "Tara, you have leaves in your hair," I said.

"So do you."

"Huh?" I brushed fat leaves and chunks of dried mud from my hair. How did we get so dirty?

The clouds parted. Pale silver moonlight poured over us.

I shivered again. "Do you have your cell?" I asked. "Call Mom and Dad. Tell them we're a little late."

Tara reached into her backpack and pulled out

her cell phone. "You're such a *good* boy, Nicky. Always thinking of Mom and Dad." She pinched my cheek really hard.

I hate that. And she knows it.

I slapped her arm. "Touched you last."

She slapped me back. "Touched *you* last."

"No. Touched *you* last."

I tried to dodge her hand and crashed into a tree.

Tara laughed.

"That's cruel," I said. "Why do you always laugh when I hurt myself?"

"Because it's funny?"

Actually, it didn't hurt at all. My head slammed into the tree trunk and I didn't even feel it.

Tara slapped my shoulder. "Touched you last."

"That's enough," I said. "Call Mom and Dad."

Some of our "touched you last" games go on for hours. Once we played it in the backseat during a long car trip. We played until Dad pulled over to the side of the road and started pounding his head against the steering wheel, begging us to stop.

Tara squinted as she punched in the phone number. "Nicky, it's so dark, I can't even see what time it is," she said. "But it must be really late."

We walked past big houses that had wide front lawns littered with dead leaves. A grinning jack-o'-lantern stared out at us from a living room window.

"Is it Halloween already?" I asked. "School hasn't started yet, has it?" I shut my eyes and tried to think. I had a cold feeling at the back of my neck. Why couldn't I remember if school had started?

Tara had her phone pressed to her ear. After a few seconds, she lowered it. She shook it hard. "Dead," she said, holding it up to show me. "How can it be dead? I just charged it. At least, I think I did."

She shoved the phone into her backpack and pulled out her Walkman. Tara is an electronics freak. She's the only fourth grader at Jefferson Elementary with a cell phone, a pager, and a PalmPilot.

Mom and Dad finally got me a laptop for my eleventh birthday, after I begged for months. But they spoil Tara like crazy because she's the baby of the family.

Last Christmas, they asked Tara what she wanted. And she said, "A charge card at Circuit City." They didn't get it for her. But they thought it was cool that she asked.

Mom and Dad think it's great that Tara likes all those gadgets. Because Mom and Dad both work with a lot of gadgets. They both . . . uh . . . they work together on . . . uh . . .

Weird. How come I can't remember what Mom and Dad do?

Why can't I remember anything tonight? What's wrong with me?

We turned onto Bleek Street. We live at 143 Bleek. I couldn't wait to get to our nice warm house. A car rolled past slowly. I recognized Mr. Carter, one of our neighbors. I waved to him, but he didn't turn his head or wave back or anything.

"We're almost home. Why are you putting on your Walkman?" I asked Tara.

"So I don't have to talk to you," she answered.

Nice.

After a few seconds, she tore the headphones off. "This is dead too," she said. "I know I always keep in fresh batteries. But it's totally dead. Nicky, what's going on?"

I shrugged. I had that cold feeling at the back of my neck again. I was starting to feel a little scared, but I didn't want Tara to know.

She shook the Walkman and pushed some buttons. Then, with a sigh, she shoved it into the backpack. "I hope Mom and Dad kept dinner warm," she said. "I'm kinda hungry."

We crossed the street. One block from home. The wind howled around the Fosters' house on the corner, pushing us back.

"Look out!" Tara screamed.

We both leaped off the sidewalk as two boys came roaring past us on skateboards. Tara fell to the grass, and I landed in the Fosters' hedge.

"Whoa!" I didn't recognize the boys. They both wore purple and gray Jefferson High jackets and baggy cargo jeans.

Tara jumped to her feet. "Hey—what's your problem?" she shouted after them.

They totally ignored her.

Tara doesn't like to be ignored. She tore after them, screaming for them to stop.

"Hey, wait," I said. "Let 'em go." I tried to hold her back.

She slipped out of my grasp and plowed into one of the boys from behind. He tumbled into his friend, and they both went sailing to the sidewalk. Clattering loudly, their skateboards rolled into the street and came to a stop at the curb.

"Guess you wiped out!" Tara said.

"Hey, why'd you do that?" One of the guys shoved his friend.

"You fell into *me*!" the other one cried. "Maybe you should try a scooter."

They shoved each other for a while. Then they climbed back onto their boards and took off.

I hurried up to Tara. "You okay?"

She tilted her head to one side and twisted her mouth the way she always does when she's worried about something. "Yeah. I guess. But how come they ignored us? It was like they didn't see us."

I shrugged. I couldn't explain it. But I said,

"You know. High school guys. They *never* see us. We're just kids, right?"

The wind howled again, and the moon disappeared behind the clouds. "L-let's get home," I said, shivering. My legs had goose bumps up and down them.

Why was I wearing shorts in October? Was it warm this morning? Why couldn't I remember?

We began walking again. Tara adjusted the backpack on her shoulders. She still had that tight, worried look on her face. "Nicky, can I ask you a question?"

"Yeah. Okay."

"Well . . . where are we coming from?"

I turned and stared at her. Her long plastic earrings were rattling in the wind. Mom wanted Tara to wait till sixth grade to get her ears pierced. But Tara never waits for anything. Mom had to give in.

"Where are we coming from?" I repeated. A black SUV roared through the stop sign and swept past us.

Tara nodded. "Yeah. That's my question."

"Well . . ." My heart started to pound. "Where are we coming from?" I shut my eyes again. Sometimes it helps me think better.

But not tonight.

"Hel-*lo*. Here we are walking home late at night," Tara said. "But where were we? Why are we out so late? Why are we dressed for summer?

Why would Mom and Dad let us walk home this late?"

I pulled a twig from my hair, one that I'd missed. "I don't know, Tara. I . . . I can't remember."

"Well, I can't either." Her voice broke. "We had to be *somewhere,* right?"

My heart pounded harder. I took a deep breath. "This is kinda scary," I whispered.

Tara nodded. "Kinda. Something is wrong with our memories. I can't remember anything."

I brushed a clump of dirt off her shoulder. "Neither can I. But at least we're close to home. Mom and Dad will help us."

We jogged the rest of the way. I kept trying to think of where we'd just come from. But I didn't have a clue. Why did I suddenly have a hole in my brain?

We were breathing hard as we jumped onto the front stoop. The porch light was on, and there was mail poking out of the mailbox.

I read the name stenciled on the box: DOYLE. A chill ran down my spine. "Doyle? Who's that? Our name is Roland. Somebody painted a new name on our mailbox." My voice came out high and choked.

Tara grabbed my arm. "I . . . I don't like this, Nicky. What's going on? I'm really scared."

I pulled my door key from my pocket. My heart was still thudding like a drum in my chest.

My hand trembled as I slid the key into the lock. "Whoa." The key stuck in the hole. I struggled to turn it. No. It wouldn't turn.

I pulled the key out and turned it upside down. No. It wouldn't slide into the lock that way either.

I turned to Tara, who huddled close at my side. "My key . . . it doesn't work."

She stared back at me, her gray-green eyes wide with fright. "Nicky, I'm scared."

"Me too," I admitted. "But I'm sure Mom and Dad will explain everything."

Tara sighed. "I hope." She raised her finger and pushed the doorbell. "Mom? Dad? Are you there? It's us!"

2

I HEARD FOOTSTEPS. THE knob turned from inside. And then the door swung open.

A woman I'd never seen before stuck her head out. She was short and thin, with wavy black hair and dark eyes behind red plastic glasses.

"Hello—?" I said.

She glanced all around as if she didn't see Tara and me.

"Who are you?" Tara asked. "Are our parents home?"

Squinting behind the red-framed glasses, she gazed right over my shoulder.

"Harriet? Who is it?" a man called from the living room.

Not Dad's voice. A stranger.

"It's us. Nicky and Tara. We live here," I said.

"There's no one here, John," the woman named Harriet replied. She frowned and shook her head.

"Well, someone rang the bell," John called in a booming voice. "I heard it."

"Probably some kids playing Halloween tricks early."

"Friends of Max's," a boy with a deep voice said. "My friends wouldn't be that stupid."

"My friends aren't stupid, Colin!" I heard another boy shout.

"You don't *have* any friends!" the first boy said.

"Uh . . . excuse me—?" I tried one more time.

But the woman started to close the door.

"Hey!" Tara cried. She ducked inside and I slipped in after her.

"Oh, wow!" I uttered a startled cry. It was our house, okay. But our furniture was gone. Everything was different. I saw a brown leather couch where our two big armchairs had stood. And a wide-screen TV where Dad had his exercise bike.

Tara grabbed my arm and held on tightly. "This is too weird, Nicky. I'm not happy right now. Who *are* these people?"

A cold shiver ran down my back. I realized I was trembling. "They don't see us," I whispered. "And they don't hear us."

Tara gripped my arm harder. "Do you think they're ghosts or something? Remember that movie about the haunted house? The ghosts thought *they* were the ones who were alive. They didn't realize they were ghosts."

I remembered that movie. It totally creeped me

out. I had nightmares for a week—even when I was awake!

Now I felt sick. Like I might puke. My stomach was churning and my throat tightened till I could barely breathe.

I held my breath, trying not to toss up my lunch. I watched the family in *our* living room. They were all standing. They seemed to be in the middle of an argument.

The dad stood behind the couch. He was a big beefy guy. He had a red face and a shiny bald head except for a strip of black hair that curved around from ear to ear.

He wore a Grateful Dead T-shirt over baggy khakis. A red and blue tattoo of a fire-breathing dragon glowed on his right bicep.

The mom looked tiny and frail standing next to him. She wore gray sweats and kept fiddling nervously with the hem of her shirt.

Two boys stood near the window. One was tall and athletic-looking. All puffed up with abs of steel. He looked as if he worked out at least twenty hours a day.

He had short, spikey blond hair, blue eyes, and a dimple in each cheek. He wore a plaid flannel shirt open over a black T-shirt, and tight-fitting, faded jeans, torn at the knees. He was the older brother, I decided—thirteen or fourteen. The one named Colin.

Max didn't resemble his older brother much. He was eleven or twelve, average height, and a little chubby. He had a bird's nest of black curly hair on top of a round sort-of baby face.

He wore a *Matrix* T-shirt over baggy cargo khakis. He kept clenching and unclenching his fists.

"I don't think the Plover School is the right place for Max," the mom said. She had a tweety, birdlike voice that kept trilling up and down. "Max is a sensitive boy."

Colin tossed back his head and laughed. "Sensitive? Is that another word for helpless wimp?"

"Don't call your brother names," the mom said.

Max stuck his tongue out at Colin. "It's very rude to call people names, you stupid idiot."

Colin raised his fist at Max. Max tried to hide behind his tiny mother.

"Max is kinda cute," Tara whispered. "In a geeky sort of way."

Colin grinned at his brother. "They make you march all day at the Plover School. In the hot sun. Most of the guys faint from heat exhaustion. A few kids drop dead every year, but they don't think that's a big deal." He laughed again.

"I can't go to a school with uniforms," Max said. "You know I'm allergic to starch."

"I went to the Plover School, and I loved

every minute," the dad boomed. "It turned me into a man. It will do the same for you. You'll be strong and athletic and popular, like Colin. And you won't bring home any more report cards like this." He waved a sheet of paper in the air.

"But Max got straight As," his mother protested.

"He's failing phys ed," Mr. Doyle said. "I can't have a son of mine fail phys ed. Look at him. Day and night at his computer. He never works out. He doesn't have a girlfriend."

"Dad—I'm eleven!" Max cried.

Mr. Doyle shook his head. "Colin is right. I hate to say it, Max, but you're a wimp. And now you're seeing ghosts everywhere in the house. Making up crazy ghost stories."

"I don't make them up. They're *true!*" Max said. "There's a ghost in the kitchen! I hear it late at night!"

"The Plover School will take care of your ghosts, Max," Mr. Doyle said. "I'm doing it for your own good. Now, stop arguing. Here. Let's all go outside and toss the ball around."

Colin picked up a football and started toward the door.

"Dad, it's night. It's too dark," Max said. "And I hate that football. It's too pointy. Last time, I had bruises all over my chest."

Colin stepped back and raised the ball. "Max—think fast!" He heaved the ball into Max's stomach.

The ball bounced away. Max let out a groan and doubled over in pain.

The mom rushed over and threw her arms around him. "You leave Maxie alone!" she shouted at Colin.

Colin laughed. "Sorry, Maxie. I thought you could catch it."

Max groaned again and struggled to stand up straight. He raised his fists toward Colin. "You want a piece of me? Come on. You want a piece of me?"

That made everyone laugh.

"That's what the Plover School will do for you," Mr. Doyle said. "Make you strong enough to take on your brother."

"Let's go, Dad," Colin said. He picked up the ball. He and his father jogged out the door.

"Max is funny," Tara whispered. "Why would they want to send him away?"

I shrugged. "We can't worry about Max. We've got big-time problems of our own."

I pointed to the mirror over the mantel. Tara followed my gaze. I could see Max and his mom reflected very clearly in the mirror. *But where were Tara and I?*

Not there.

Tara crossed the room and stepped up close to the mirror. She waved her hands in front of it.

No reflection.

When she turned back to me, she had tears in her eyes. "We're invisible," she choked out. "They can't see us or hear us because..."

She couldn't say it.

I couldn't say it either. I kept swallowing and swallowing. My mouth felt as dry as burnt toast. I had a frightening, cold feeling all over.

Finally, I said, "Because... *we're* ghosts? We're the ghosts here, Tara, haunting our own house."

She wiped the tears off her cheeks. Tara was tough. She never cried. Never. Not even when Potsy, our dog, was run over.

"How can we be ghosts?" she asked. "I don't remember dying, and we were shivering outside in the cold, right? And I'm starving right now. Ghosts don't get cold or hungry, do they?"

I stared at her. "How should I know? I've never been a ghost before!"

"What do we do now, Nicky?" Her voice broke.

"I don't know," I whispered. I started to feel very strange... weak. "Tara..."

A thick gray mist filled the room. Max and his mom disappeared behind the mist. I couldn't hear their voices anymore.

"Nicky—I'm fading." I heard Tara's frightened whisper. "I'm fading away . . . disappearing."

"Me too," I choked out. I struggled to hold on. But something was pulling me away . . . away . . .

"Goodbye," I whispered to my sister.

"Goodbye."

I could barely hear her reply.

3

WHY DOES DAD MAKE such a big deal about phys ed? I got straight As this semester. I always get straight As. The kids call me Max the Brainimon because I'm the brainiest guy in my class. But Dad doesn't care about brains.

That football hit me so hard in the gut, I thought I was going to toss my dinner on the couch. And what did Dad do? He laughed.

Ha, ha. What a riot. Dad thinks if he throws enough footballs at me, I'll start to want to learn how to catch them. But I won't.

What I'd really love to do is heave the ball into Colin's gut. I'd love to see the look on his face. Well . . . actually, he probably wouldn't have a look on his face. Baboons don't have expressions, do they?

He probably wouldn't even feel it. He's always in his room with those workout tapes of his. *Perfect Abs. Stomach of Steel. Buns of Titanium.*

He has to spend all that time on his body

because there's no point in developing a brain that small.

Ha, ha.

Dad thinks Colin is so perfect. Just because he stars in three sports, he's really popular with girls, and has a million friends.

Big deal.

Okay. He's perfect. Colin is perfect.

But there's more to life than being perfect, isn't there?

How about being nice to your little brother?

Could he pass a *Lord of the Rings* trivia test? No way.

Has he reached Level Seven in *Tomb Raider V* on PlayStation?

Does he know how Houdini did his famous straitjacket escape? Does he know how any of the great magicians did their tricks? No. But I do.

There's a lot Colin doesn't know.

Why do I have to go to the Plover School? So *what* if Dad loved it so much? Maybe I don't *want* to go to a school that will make a man out of me. I'm eleven! I don't want to be a man yet!

I was so steamed, I wanted to punch the wall. But I knew I had to be careful. I need my hands for my magic tricks. Besides, I'd probably cut myself, and I hate the sight of blood.

Can Colin make a live pigeon disappear?

Can he?

I don't think so.

At school, I've been spreading the rumor that Colin wets the bed every night. It isn't true, but so what? I think at least a couple people believe me.

And Dad is wrong. I *do* have friends. Well, I have one good friend—Aaron.

But Mom and Dad don't want me to be friends with Aaron. They think he's weird. Hey, what's wrong with being a little weird?

Okay, okay. So he wears swim goggles to school every day. He needs glasses, so he had prescription lenses put into them. A little oddball, maybe, but who are they to judge?

He does some other strange things too. For one thing, he never does his homework. He says it takes too much time away from watching TV.

On Career Day, Aaron wrote that he plans to study to be a superhero and fight crime everywhere in the universe. He got an F on that paper, and his parents had to go in for a conference.

Aaron is a little whacked, okay? But he's also a really good friend.

What can I do? I can't let Dad send me to that school. I can't go to a school where you have to wear an ugly gray uniform. I look terrible in gray.

Yes, sir. No, sir. Yes, ma'am. They turn kids into robots at the Plover School. Aaron and I are going to make a video about kids who get turned into robots. But I don't want the movie to be my life story!

I *can't* let them send me there!

Okay, okay, Max. Easy, boy.

When I'm totally steamed, practicing my magic tricks is the only thing that will settle me down. It works because I have to concentrate really hard on what I'm doing. So I forget about Dad and Big Dude Colin and all my other problems.

I'm going to perform at the Halloween party at school. So I've got to get my act together. No slipups. I want everyone to think my act is really cool.

I mean, I'm not exactly in the cool group at school. I guess I'm not in any group at all. Aaron and I can't be a group on our own, can we?

I'm not the best magician in the world yet. But I'm working on it.

Mom even bought me a white pigeon to practice the disappearing trick with. I named him Joey, and I keep him in a nice big cage near the window so he can see the sunlight.

Making Joey disappear right from my hands is my best trick. And it's the hardest to perform. Mainly because I have to make Joey slide down my jacket sleeve so fast that no one sees it.

I pulled on my black magician's jacket with the extra-wide sleeves. Then I crossed the room to the window. "Hi, Joey."

Joey tilted his head at me, staring up with one eye. I lifted him carefully out of the cage with both hands. He warbled. I could feel it come from deep in his throat.

"We're going to practice our trick, Joey." He warbled some more. Did he enjoy the trick? I couldn't tell. He never tried to fly away. Maybe that meant he was happy.

"Hold very still," I told him. "That's your whole job, holding still."

I cupped Joey in the palms of my hands. "And now, ladies and gentlemen," I started in my deep, magician's voice.

But before I could go any further, a cold rush of wind brushed past me.

"Boo!" a voice screamed.

And an ice-cold hand gripped the back of my neck.

4

"AAAAIIH!" I SCREAMED. JOEY fluttered to the floor.

The hand let go. I spun around.

Colin hunched over me with a disgusting happy grin on his face. "Gotcha, Freak Face."

I took a step back. "You are *so* not funny." I rubbed the back of my neck. "Why is your hand so cold?"

His grin grew wider. "I kept it in the freezer for fifteen minutes."

My mouth dropped open. "Just to scare me?"

He snickered. "Yeah. Did you think it was one of those ghosts you've been hearing ever since we moved in here?"

"No," I lied. There was no point in talking about the ghost. I know I hear something late at night in the kitchen, but he'll never believe me.

I bent down to pick up Joey, but Colin got there first. He tightened his fingers around the pigeon and raised him high in the air so I couldn't reach him.

"Give him back!" I shouted. I gave Colin a hard shove, but he didn't budge.

"I need him," Colin said.

"What for?"

"For dog food. I'm going to feed him to Buster." He laughed as if that was the funniest joke in the world.

"Give him back! He's mine!" I screamed. I jumped as high as I could, but I couldn't reach Joey.

"I'll bet pigeon tastes just like chicken," Colin said. "You know Buster likes chicken." Holding the pigeon in his tight fist, Colin started for the door.

"Give him back to me!" I screamed, chasing after Colin. I tried to tackle him, but I slid right off. What was that ripping sound? Did I tear my magician's jacket?

"You can't do this! You can't!" I wailed.

Colin turned at the door. "Want to save Joey's life?"

"Yes," I said, climbing to my feet. "If you haven't already squeezed him to death."

"Okay. Walk Buster for a week," Colin said.

"You're joking!" I cried.

Buster is our big furry wolfhound. We adopted him from the pound a couple of years ago, and we keep him mainly in the garage and backyard. He hates me. The minute he sees me, he starts growling and snapping. I don't know why. Maybe he senses that I really wanted a Chihuahua.

"That's the deal," Colin said, holding Joey up. "Walk Buster for a week—or the bird is doggy dinner."

"But—but—" I sputtered. "Last week, Buster tried to chew my leg off!"

Colin shrugged. "Maybe *you* taste like chicken." He squeezed Joey tighter. "Deal?"

I stared at the little pigeon, his little head poking out of Colin's fist. "Deal," I said.

I could see Buster's eyes glowing in the darkness of the garage. I clicked on the light and raised the leather leash. "Walk, Buster? Go for a walk?"

The huge dog ducked his head and uttered a low growl.

"Good boy," I lied. "Good boy. Go for a walk."

I took a step toward the dog. My legs were kinda shaky. Why am I doing this? I wondered. I had to remind myself I was saving a pigeon's life.

To my surprise, Buster loped up to me and lowered his head so I could put on the leash. "Good boy. Good boy," I kept repeating. "Please don't bite my face off tonight. I want to look good for the class photographs."

The dog nodded as if he understood. I clicked the leash onto his collar. He gave a hard tug, eager to get outside and do his business.

I let him lead me out of the garage, down the driveway, and into the street. He raised his leg at the tree stump at the bottom of the drive, one of his favorite places. Then we walked on toward the corner.

It was a cool October night. Gusts of wind sent brittle dead leaves swirling down the street. The moon had disappeared behind low black clouds.

Buster loped along, sniffing the grass, sniffing a pile of leaves, sniffing everything. I think to dogs, sniffing is like reading. They can't read, so they sniff everything instead.

I let Buster sniff whatever he wanted. I was so happy that he wasn't snarling and trying to turn me into a dog biscuit.

It all went fine until we reached the corner.

We stepped into the circle of yellow light from the streetlamp, and Buster started to change.

He stopped suddenly and turned his big furry head to me.

I leaned down. "Buster, what's wrong?"

Then the dog opened his mouth—as if to speak!

As I stared in shock, his mouth opened wider. His black lips pulled back until I could see all his teeth. The lips pulled back farther. The mouth pulled open even wider.

"Buster—?"

I gasped in horror as the lips pulled back . . .

back . . . until Buster's whole head disappeared. Was he *swallowing* himself?

His eyes disappeared inside his skin. The gaping mouth slid back over Buster's body. I could see glistening wet, pink flesh—the insides of his throat.

And then, as the fur peeled back, I saw pale bones and gleaming yellow and red organs. Buster's purple, pulsing heart. His rib cage. His balloonlike stomach. His twisting yellow guts.

"Ohhh." My stomach churned as I stared, frozen in horror.

Blood shot through purple, pulsing veins. Buster's heart throbbed *outside* his body. Gloppy, half-digested food fell from his stomach and plopped onto the sidewalk.

In seconds, he stood in front of me—*inside out*!

Only his wagging tail remained covered with fur. The rest of him pulsed and throbbed and glistened, his wet and shiny insides *on the outside*.

"Ohh." I let out another groan. I pressed a hand over my mouth, trying to keep my dinner down. My whole body shook.

How could this be happening? I glanced around quickly. Was anyone else nearby? Was I the only one seeing this?

The houses were all dark. No one else was on the street.

Something moved from inside the bulging, pink

dog stomach. A shadow formed. A wisp of black mist floated up from the panting inside-out dog.

Under the streetlamp, the black mist rose quickly, and spread.

And in the swirling fog, I saw the figure of a man.

I dropped to my knees in fright and stared helplessly as the man formed, lifting himself slowly. His face was hidden in darkness. His body was wrapped in a flowing black cloak down to his ankles.

The figure shifted and swayed in the swirling black fog. I huddled beside Buster and stared up as the shadowy figure floated over me.

And in a booming voice, so powerful it made the grass quiver and bend, he said:

"Where are they? Tell me where they are, and I might let you live!"

5

"WHOA—! PLEASE—" I JUMPED to my feet and tried to back away. But I tripped over the curb and landed on my butt on the grass.

The fog swirled over me, pinning me to the ground. Inside the mist, I could see the man in the swirling cloak.

"Tell me!" he screamed.

His breath was a rush of hot wind, putrid like rotten fish. The stench hung over me. I held my breath, waiting for it to fade away.

"Tell me where they are!" Again, the hot, smelly breath roared over me.

"Who—? Where?" I choked out. "I—I really don't know what you're talking about."

"Don't lie to me, fool!"

A wisp of black fog shot over my arm. I let out a scream as sharp pain stabbed through my hand.

"No—oh, please!" I uttered a weak cry as the skin began to peel back from my fingers. My fingernails flopped loosely.

"Ohhh. It hurts! It really hurts!" I could see all

the blue veins and yellow tendons and muscles of my hand.

I opened and closed my fist, trying to lessen the pain. I watched the tendons and muscles move, the tiny veins pulsing with blood. Stab after stab of fiery pain shot up my hand, my arm, my whole body.

"See what I can do?" the voice boomed, sending another spray of hot, fish-stinking breath over me.

"Yes," I whispered, gaping at my ugly, wet claw. "Please—it hurts so much. . . ."

A wave of his shadowy arm, and the skin slid back over my hand. It moved over my fingers like a tight-fitting glove. The fingernails pulled back into place.

"Next time I won't be so nice. Next time, I will peel you like an orange."

Shaking, I tried to move my fingers. They seemed to work okay.

This can't be happening, I told myself. My hand still ached. *Please, Max—wake up from this nightmare.*

I stared at the figure, hidden in the black cloak. *Who is he?* I wondered, struggling to stop my body from shaking. *What does he want with me?*

"Now, tell me where they are!" the voice boomed.

"I . . . really don't understand," I said, gazing up at the billowing figure in the fog. "Who are you?"

"My name is Phears. I am the Animal-Traveler."

I climbed to my knees. "You . . . travel inside animals?" My voice trembled.

"Stop stalling," he rasped, floating over me like a black cloud. "I've been in your room. I couldn't find them. Where are you hiding them?"

"You . . . you've been in my room?"

"They might as well surrender." Phears ignored my question. "Their parents are gone for good. And we, their prisoners, have all escaped. All the ghosts are out."

"Huh? I—I can't help you. I don't know what you're talking about," I said, my teeth chattering. "I'm not hiding anyone. I'm just here walking my inside-out dog."

"You're lying!" he screamed. His hot breath blasted me, so putrid I couldn't breathe. "Say your final prayer!"

"No—please! Please! I'm not hiding anyone. You got the wrong guy! Did you try my neighbors?"

The thick fog floated over me. A roar filled my ears. I stared up at the shadowy figure. The darkness swirled tightly around me, circling me, smothering me.

I grabbed my throat. It felt as if someone was squeezing my neck . . . tighter . . . tighter . . .

I squirmed and ducked and dodged, but I couldn't escape the choking grip on my throat.

This isn't fair, I thought. *He's got the wrong guy... the wrong guy. I'm going to die—and it's all a mistake.*

Gasping, wheezing, I struggled for breath. My chest burned. The ground swayed beneath me. I fell to the grass. Everything started to spin.

I couldn't fight it. Couldn't breathe.

Finally, I gave up and surrendered to the fog, surrendered to the hot, black, choking wind.

6

BRIGHT LIGHT WASHED OVER the darkness. I blinked.

I must have passed out for a moment. I was still on my knees on the corner.

The light split in two. I blinked again and a car came into focus. It turned the corner, and the beam from its twin headlights rolled over me.

Phears floated above me. The light swept right through him. He let out a hoarse gasp. I saw his hands fly up to protect his face as if the light was painful to him. Twisting away from the glow, he curled into a tight ball. Then he disappeared into his fog, and the fog vanished too.

Phears can't stand light, I realized.

I turned to Buster—still inside out. He was lying on his side in the grass. His purple heart was pounding hard. It made a *slicccck slicccck slicccck* sound, sort of like windshield wipers.

"Hey, Max—" The car stopped. Mrs. Murray, one of our neighbors, poked her head out the driver's window.

"Oh. Hi, Mrs. Murray." I climbed to my feet, feeling shaky and dazed. Phears' terrifying voice still boomed in my ears.

Mrs. Murray pointed to Buster. "Did you drop your garbage there? Need help picking it up?"

"No thanks," I said. "It's just my dog."

Her mouth dropped open. She raised her eyes from Buster to me. "You're such a strange boy, Max," she said. The car roared away.

I shook my head, trying to clear it. What just happened? Did I really see what I thought I saw?

I couldn't stop trembling. My legs felt like rubber bands. My breath rattled in my throat.

It had to be a hidden-camera TV show, right? And now people were going to come jumping out of the bushes, telling me how scared I looked and how hilarious the whole thing was.

But no. No cameras. No hidden TV crew in the bushes.

It really happened. Who was Phears? Some kind of ghost or zombie or something? Why did he travel inside animals? And why did he think I was hiding someone from him?

He said he had been in my room. That thought sent a chill down my back. And he said next time he'd peel me like an orange.

Oh, wow. I had to make sure there *was* no next time. But—how?

I squeezed my hand. The skin was back nice

and tight. I shuddered and pictured it all peeled again with the yellow tendons and blue veins showing.

At least Phears is gone, I thought.

But I was wrong.

As I turned to Buster, the black cloud floated over me again. I blinked, struggling to see in the heavy mist. And once again, I heard Phears' booming voice.

"I know Nicky and Tara Roland are back," he said. "And I know you are hiding them."

I raised my hands to shield myself. "Please—no more pain. You've made a big mistake."

"You are the one making the mistake," Phears boomed from inside his ghostly fog. "But I am leaving now. I am clouding your mind so you will not remember me. I don't want you to warn them. I don't want them to know that I am coming. So I am erasing your memory for now. But don't worry—I will be back!"

Everything went bright red for a minute. So bright, I had to shut my eyes.

When I opened them, I was standing on the street corner with Buster's leash in my hand. Why did my hand ache? Had Buster snapped at me?

I gazed around the dark street. Something had just happened, I knew. Something strange. I struggled to remember. I felt kinda shaky and weak.

But I couldn't remember anything strange.

Buster bared his teeth and started to growl at me. He swung his head around and tried to take a bite out of my leg. At least *he* felt totally normal.

I tugged him home and locked him up in the garage. Then I hurried inside, still feeling weird.

I found Mom and Dad in the den, side by side on the brown leather couch, staring at the wide-screen TV. "What took you so long, Maxie?" Mom asked, her eyes straight ahead on the screen.

"I . . . don't know," I answered. "I feel kinda dizzy, kinda weak. And my hand hurts."

"Hold it down!" Dad snapped. "Wrestling is on." He leaned toward the TV screen so that his face was nearly in the ring with the two hulky wrestlers.

"Max, you'd better go up to your room," Mom said. "You're interrupting a grudge match."

"Aren't they *all* grudge matches?" I asked.

They didn't hear me. They were cheering on one of the wrestlers, shouting and shaking their fists in the air. Mom was usually so quiet, like a little mouse. But she enjoyed wrestling more than Dad.

"Kill him! *Kill* him!" she was screaming.

Dad slapped her a hard high five.

I turned and climbed the stairs to my room.

I IM'd Aaron for an hour or so. I was starting to feel more normal. I asked Aaron if he had trouble with the algebra homework. Some of the equations were about a mile long.

But, of course, Aaron hadn't opened his math book. He never does.

That's one reason I really like Aaron. He's just about the only kid in my class who never asks me for help with his homework!

Other kids call me all the time. "Brainimon, help me with my science project."

"Brainimon, what's the answer to number six?"

"Please, Brainimon—write a quick book report for me."

My phone rings so often, you'd think I was actually popular!

Anyway, I was online with Aaron until nearly eleven. Then, yawning, I tucked myself into bed. I could hear Colin playing his guitar in his room down the hall. After a while, the music stopped.

I had nearly drifted off to sleep when I heard the noises in the kitchen. Again. The scraping sounds. The clanging of pots. Faint footsteps.

And then the soft croak of a voice. Soft and sad, like a sigh.

"Oh, glory. Oh, glory..."

Trembling, I jammed the pillow over my head and covered my ears.

I didn't want to hear these ghostly whispers. I'd heard them every night, ever since we moved into this house. No one else heard them. No one believed me.

Who was down there? If only I had the courage to go and see . . .

Instead, I jammed the pillow over my head—and prayed whoever it was would go away.

7

THE NEXT FEW DAYS went by without any problems. Except two kids dropped out of my afterschool *Stargate SG-1* club. They said *Stargate SG-1* was boring, and they wanted to join a *Deep Space Nine* club instead.

"The joke is on them," Aaron said after they left. "There *is* no *Deep Space Nine* Club. It broke up three years ago."

So now there was just Aaron and me left in the *Stargate SG-1* club. Kinda boring, since we're not into *Stargate SG-1* that much. We just wanted to make some new friends.

On Monday afternoon, I hurried home and hard-boiled eight eggs. They were almost finished when Colin came nosing around. "Yo. What's up, Chicken Lips?" he asked, staring into the pot.

"Just making some eggs," I said.

He started to reach into the boiling water to pull one out. I knew what he planned to do. Drop the egg into my T-shirt pocket and then smash it. He'd done it before.

Luckily, his phone rang, and he hurried to answer it.

A close call.

Why did I need eight hard-boiled eggs? For juggling, of course. Juggling is an important part of my magic act. I don't want to be a good juggler. I want to be an *awesome* juggler.

That night after dinner, I took my eggs out of the fridge, went up to my room, closed the door, and began to practice in front of the mirror. I juggled four eggs at once, keeping two in the air at all times.

Yes. Yes!

I really had a good rhythm going.

And then I heard a voice, a whispered voice behind me: *"We're back—!"*

I stared into the mirror. No one was there.

I spun around. No one.

I started juggling again. Two eggs up, two down. Two eggs up . . .

And then another whispered voice—so close to me I could feel a rush of cold wind on the back of my neck. *"Yes, we're back."*

The hard-boiled eggs flew out of my hands.

"Ow—!"

One egg cracked and splattered on my head. The yolk ran down my forehead. Another egg cracked on my sneaker, spreading yellow goo over the laces.

Big jerk Colin. *He switched the eggs!*

Wiping egg yolk off my face, I stared at a boy and a girl. They both wore short-sleeved T-shirts even though it was freezing outside, and straight-legged, faded jeans.

"How—? How did you—" I sputtered.

How did they get in my bedroom? Who were they? How come I could *see right through them*?

They were both tall and thin, with slender, serious faces. The boy had spikey brown hair and seemed to be about my age—eleven.

The girl wore a floppy red hat, so I couldn't see her face very well. She had matching red plastic earrings dangling from her ears. She looked about nine or ten.

The girl blinked as if just waking up. "We're back, Nicky," she repeated to the boy.

"I was so frightened," the boy said. "I thought we had faded away forever."

"Who are you?" I tried to shout, but my voice caught in my throat.

"That boy Max is still here," the girl said, narrowing her eyes at me.

"How long have we been gone?" the boy asked.

She shrugged. "I don't know. But, look—he's still wearing the same clothes. He should lose the baggy cargo pants. They make him look like a sailboat."

"What's with the egg dripping down his face?" the boy asked. "Tara, are you sure we're not having a crazy nightmare?"

She grabbed his arm. "This is too scary. Make him go away."

"Who are you?" I finally managed to shout. One of the four eggs hadn't broken. I picked it up to use as a weapon. "What are you doing in my room?"

"*Your* room? It's *my* room!" the boy named Nicky shouted.

"Whoa. Nicky." Tara's mouth dropped open. She tugged at the sides of her floppy red hat. "Nicky, that boy—he . . . he can *see* us!"

"Yes, I can see you!" I cried. "But I don't want to! Get out. Get out of here!"

"We're starting to fade again," Tara said. "Nicky, I'm afraid. I can feel myself disappearing again."

"We've got to learn to control this," Nicky said. He turned to me. "Being a ghost isn't as easy as it looks, Max."

Then they both disappeared.

My legs were trembling so hard, I grabbed the side of my desk to hold myself up. I glanced around the room frantically. My heart pounded like crazy.

"Are you gone?" I cried. "Did you leave?"

"We're still here," Nicky said. "I'm sitting on your bed. I mean, *my* bed. This *is* my room, you know."

"You can hear us," Tara said. "No one else can. Only you."

"Yes, I can hear you. But I can't see you now. You're invisible. Please—you're scaring me to death. Go away," I pleaded. "I'm afraid of ghosts. No kidding."

"You *should* be afraid of us," Nicky said.

"Why?" I asked in a tiny voice.

Nicky lowered his voice. "Because we're going to haunt you forever," he whispered.

8

THEY BOTH LAUGHED HIGH, evil laughs.

I felt a whiff of cold air.

"Mom! Dad!" I began to scream at the top of my lungs. "Help me! Mom! Dad!"

Maybe the wrestling show was over. Maybe they could hear me downstairs.

I turned and saw the extra eggs rising up from the bowl. They floated in the air in a straight line and began to circle me.

Again, the two ghosts cackled with glee. "We're going to haunt you, Maxie," the invisible girl whispered. "Haunt you forever. As long as you live in this house."

"Haunt you forever... Haunt you forever...," they both chanted.

"Mom! Dad! Hurry!" The eggs danced around me. "Somebody—help!"

"Maxie?" Colin came bursting into the room.

The four eggs dropped to the floor and splattered onto my white carpet. I leaped back against the wall, shivering in fright.

"What's up with the eggs?" Colin asked, gazing at the yellow goo spreading over the carpet. "Why did you do that?"

"I—I—I—" I stammered.

Colin stared at me. "Have you totally lost it?"

"I didn't do it!" I sputtered. "Ghosts did it! Two ghosts. A boy and a girl. They're in this room, Colin. They smashed the eggs."

Colin laughed. "Yeah, sure. Tell me another one."

Nicky and Tara suddenly reappeared. They stood in front of my bed, their arms crossed in front of their chests. They watched Colin and me with smiles on their faces.

"There they are!" I shouted, pointing. "Don't you see them?"

Colin spun around. "Yes," he said. "Yes, I see them. Right there. A boy and a girl."

I let out a startled cry. "Awesome! You *do* see them? No lie?"

"No lie," he said. "And I see Peter Pan, too! And check it out—there's Bugs Bunny. Hi, Bugs! Where's Daffy?"

"Ha, ha," Tara said. "Colin is a joker, isn't he, Nicky? Remind me to laugh later."

"He's about as funny as being dead," Nicky said.

"Colin—did you hear that?" I asked. "Did you hear Nicky and Tara?"

Colin squinted at me. "You're making up names for your invisible ghosts? Have you gone totally mental?"

"Colin can't see us, but Max can," Nicky said. "Weird."

"My arm!" Colin suddenly cried, jerking his arm back. "Help! The ghosts have control of my arm!" He punched me hard in the stomach.

"Ohhh." Pain shot through my body. Gasping for breath, I stumbled to the floor.

Colin laughed. "I didn't do it! The ghosts made me do it!"

Mom and Dad came rushing in. "What's going on? Colin—what are you doing in here?" Dad demanded.

"Helping Max with his homework," Colin said.

Then Mom and Dad saw the yellow goo running down my hair—and broken eggshells and yolk splattered all over the rug. Mom raised her hands to the sides of her face. "Who made this horrible mess?"

"I didn't do it!" I cried, my voice cracking. "My room is haunted. Two ghosts are here! Don't you see them? They're both by the door!" I pointed frantically.

Mom and Dad turned to the door. Nicky and Tara stuck their tongues out at them. Mom and Dad turned back to me.

"Maxie, you're too old to have invisible friends," Mom said. "You've got to stop making up these ghost stories."

"You don't see them?"

"He's gone totally wacko," Colin said. "I tried to talk him out of this stupid ghost story, but he wouldn't listen."

Mom still had her hands pressed to her face. "Eggs all over the carpet. We have to clean this up. What's wrong with you, Max?"

"He's definitely got too much time on his hands," Dad said, shaking his head. "This is why he should be sent away to school. To make him forget these dopey ghost stories."

"Let's talk about that later," Mom said.

"But just look at him," Dad said. He pointed at me—the Point of Death. He always points when he's really angry. "Invisible friends? Cracking an egg on his head? Is that healthy?"

"Dad, I didn't—"

"Give me a break." He turned and stomped out of the room.

"But my room is haunted!" I screamed after him.

Mom *tsk-tsk*ed. "Max, go get a bucket of soapy water and a sponge, and clean this mess up. Then get into the shower and wash the egg off your hair. And no more crazy talk about ghosts." She followed Dad downstairs.

Colin shook his head. "Can I give you some good advice?" he said.

I took a step back. "Advice?"

"Yeah. Here's some good advice." He punched me really hard in the stomach again.

"Owww!"

I howled and bent over, grabbing my knees and waiting for the pain to fade.

"The ghosts made me do that," Colin said. He turned and strode away.

As he reached the door, Tara stuck her foot out and tripped him.

"Huh?" Colin stumbled and fell. He landed with an *oof* on his stomach. Slowly, he raised himself to his knees and shook a fist at me.

"You're meat," he said. "You're hamburger now."

He pulled himself up with the hall railing and disappeared to his room.

Laughing, Nicky and Tara slapped each other a high five.

"Hel-*lo*. Did you hear what he said?" I gasped. "I'm hamburger. Hamburger!" I rubbed my sore stomach.

"How come you can see us, and the rest of your family can't?" Tara asked.

I shrugged. "Just lucky, I guess."

"That's a cool-looking pendant around your neck. Where did you get it?" Tara asked.

"My mom found it when we moved here," I told her. I grabbed it and tucked it back under my T-shirt. "Mom said it would bring me luck." I pulled a gob of egg from my hair. "But I don't think it's working yet."

"It looks sort of like a bullet," Tara said.

"What's inside it?" Nicky asked.

"Nothing. It doesn't open. Why are you two asking me all these questions?"

"We're bonding," Nicky said.

"I don't want to bond with you," I said. "Go away. Go haunt someone else. There are already ghosts in this house. There's no room for you."

They stared at me in silence.

"I'm no fun to haunt," I said. "Really. Have you ever seen projectile vomiting? That's what I do whenever I'm haunted."

"Cute," Nicky said.

"Did our parents sell this house to your parents?" Tara asked me. "Did you see my parents?"

"The house was empty," I said. "No one lived here."

"But—what happened to *us*?" Tara cried. Her voice broke. She turned away from me. "What happened to our family?"

"I don't know," I said. "I don't know who you are. Dad said we got the house cheap because no one was living here."

Nicky lowered his head sadly.

Tara's shoulders were moving up and down. I think she was crying.

"Hey . . . uh . . . are you still going to haunt me?" I asked again.

To my surprise, they both vanished.

9

"MAX NEEDS OUR HELP," Tara said.

I sighed. "He needs *our* help? Tara, *we're* the ones who need help. We're dead. We're ghosts. And we don't remember why or how it happened. And Mom and Dad are missing, and we may never see them again. Besides, he's beyond help. Look at him. He's eleven years old, and he still has Velcro sneakers!"

It was a few nights later. At least, I think it was a few nights. Tara and I had disappeared—faded into an emptiness—and we lost all track of time.

We were sitting on the floor with our backs resting against Max's bed. Behind us, he was asleep with his mouth wide open, snoring softly.

"Cut him some slack, Nicky," Tara said. "He's not a bad guy. And he's in trouble. His big brother is totally horrible to him. And his dad wants to send him away to school because he's not a big jock. Maybe we can help him.

"And maybe Max can help us, too," my sister said softly.

"Help us? How?"

"Help us find Mom and Dad. I don't think we can do it on our own. We keep appearing and disappearing. Sometimes we fade away for days. We can't control it. Sometimes we can pick up objects and sometimes we're too weak. Sometimes we're solid, and sometimes we're totally see-through. We're not good at being ghosts yet."

"We just need more practice," I said. "After a few weeks, we'll be able to haunt this house like pros!"

"But, Nicky—"

"We don't need Max," I said. "He's too frightened to help us. You heard what he said about projectile vomiting. How helpful is *that*?"

"That was a joke," Tara said. "He jokes a lot. Can't you tell when he's kidding?"

"I'm not in the mood for jokes," I grumbled. "I'm dead, remember. I don't need jokes anymore."

Behind us, Max stirred in his sleep. "Help," he whispered. "Help."

"Do you believe it?" I said. "He's even a wimp in his sleep!"

"We can help him be brave, Nicky," my sister insisted. "Then he can help us find Mom and Dad."

I pinched Tara's cheek. "I think you have a

crush on him. You do—don't you? You have a crush on him—big-time."

"Do not!" she cried, shoving my hand away. "Touched you last."

"Touched *you* last."

She slapped my arm. "Touched *you* last."

I let her win. "What do you like about him, Tara? His cute little baby face? His collection of sci-fi T-shirts? His goofy grin?"

"Shut up, Nicky!" Tara shouted. "I mean it. Shut up!"

"You're blushing," I said.

"Ghosts can't blush, you moron!"

"Well, if they could—" I started. But I stopped when I heard a noise. A muffled clattering sound. From downstairs.

"What was *that*?" Tara whispered.

We both listened. I heard creaking floorboards. Scraping sounds. The clatter of metal pots and pans. Was it coming from the kitchen?

I glanced at Max's clock radio. Nearly three in the morning. Who would be awake at this hour?

I climbed to my feet and pulled my sister up. We floated to the bedroom door and poked our heads into the hall.

More clattering sounds. A soft sizzle. Scrapes . . . and then a cough.

"Max said something about hearing other ghosts in the house," Tara whispered, staying close by my side. Her eyes grew wide. "Maybe it's Mom and Dad."

"In the kitchen?" I replied.

She shrugged. "It isn't anyone in the Doyle family. They're all sound asleep."

She tugged my hand. "Come on, Nicky. Let's check it out."

I held back. "But . . . what if it's some other ghost? A stranger?"

She stared at me. "Hey, you're afraid of ghosts, aren't you."

"Well . . . maybe," I confessed. "Maybe I'm a little afraid of ghosts. You know I never liked scary stuff. I always hid behind the couch whenever you and Dad rented those scary DVDs."

I heard the banging of pots down in the kitchen. Another hoarse cough. And then a soft whisper, floating on the air: *"Glory, glory . . ."*

Who could it be?

Tara tugged me harder. "Come on. Stop pulling back."

I followed her down the stairs . . . through the dark living room, pale yellow light seeping through the window from the street. To the kitchen in back . . .

Yes. Someone was definitely working in the kitchen. Working in the *dark*!

I couldn't help it. I started to shake. I suddenly felt tingly all over, gripped with fear.

Who would work in a kitchen in the middle of the night *in pitch black*?

Tara walked in ahead of me. I hurried to keep close to her. She stopped. Reached up to the wall. Clicked on the ceiling light.

And we both gasped in shock.

10

"LULU!" I CRIED.

I couldn't believe it. I stared at the woman by the stove—our housekeeper. She looked exactly the same—short and very round, white hair tied up on her head in a tight bun, her dark eyes glowing. She wore a long white apron over a gray blouse and skirt.

"Lulu!" Tara and I ran to hug her at the same time.

But our hands went right through her. "You—you're a ghost too," I whispered.

She nodded sadly. "Glory, glory. I died soon after you left. But I came back. I waited for you two," she said, her voice a breathy whisper. "I came every night to prepare your breakfast. I knew you'd return sooner or later."

She turned back to the stove. She worked a spatula over a big pan of fried eggs. The eggs weren't real. I could see right through them.

"But what happened to us?" Tara asked, tugging at Lulu's apron. "How long have we been gone?"

"A year . . . maybe two," Lulu said. Her voice was so weak, I could barely hear it over the sizzle of the eggs.

"Lulu, how did we die?" I asked. "Where are Mom and Dad?"

"So weak . . . ," she whispered. She flickered from view, then reappeared, still holding the spatula. "I can't hold on much longer. I waited for you. Waited to see you both . . ."

"Lulu, we've missed you so much!" Tara cried, hugging her again.

But the old woman disappeared in Tara's arms. A few seconds later, she was back, all gray now and out of focus. The ghostly eggs sizzled on the stove.

"Please—where are Mom and Dad?" I cried.

"Glory, it's good to see you," she whispered. "Glory, I've waited so long."

"Can you tell us?" Tara asked, grasping Lulu's free hand. "Can you tell us what happened to our family?"

"Phears," the old woman murmured, her gray eyes going wide.

"Fears?" I said. "What does that mean?"

"Phears." She spelled it for us. Then she faded away again, leaving a curl of fog in front of the stove.

Tara and I waited, staring at the spot where she had stood. A few seconds later, she reappeared. “I waited so long,” she said. She reached out with both hands to rub our cheeks. A smile spread over her ancient face.

The smile faded quickly. “Phears is the one,” she whispered. “Phears knows about your mom and dad. Your parents . . . they found the tunnel. They locked up the evil ghosts. But Phears let all the ghosts out. He knows. Phears knows.”

Tara and I squinted at one another. “Phears? Is Phears a ghost?” Tara asked.

“Is he in a tunnel somewhere?” I asked. “Please, Lulu—how can we find Phears?”

“Children, don’t step into the tunnel,” she whispered. “Only the living can go into the tunnel . . . and return.”

“Tunnel? What tunnel?” I asked. “Where can we find Phears?”

“Glory, it’s good to see you both. Glory, I’ve missed you so much.” She gave us a sad wave, then faded away. The spatula floated in midair.

“Lulu, wait!” I pleaded. “Come back. Tell us about Phears. Tell us about our parents. Please—!”

The spatula vanished. I heard the sizzle of the eggs. Then they vanished too, along with the pan.

Tara and I stared at each other, alone in the kitchen now. “Who is Phears?” Tara asked. “Why was Lulu talking about a tunnel? Why wouldn’t she tell us about Mom and Dad?”

I shrugged. "I don't know." A shiver ran down my back. "Let's wake up Max," I said. "Maybe he knows who Phears is."

We floated back upstairs. I could feel myself getting weaker. All the excitement over seeing Lulu was draining my strength. I knew I'd be fading away soon.

We hurried to Max's room. He lay sprawled on his back, mouth open, arms dangling over the sides of the bed. "Wake up, Max!" I whispered.

He didn't move, so I raised my voice. "Wake up! Come on—wake up!" I lowered my mouth to his ear and shouted, *"Wake up Max!"*

Tara grabbed him by the shoulders and started to shake him. "Wake up! Wake up!" Suddenly, she gasped and let go. His head dropped limply to the pillow.

"Oh no!" Tara cried, covering her mouth with one hand. "I can't wake him up. He's dead, Nicky. Max is *dead*!"

11

A CHILL WENT DOWN my back. I froze for a moment, staring at his limp body. "That's impossible," I whispered.

I pushed Tara out of the way and grabbed Max's shoulders. "Wake up! Max! Can you hear me? *Wake up!*"

This can't be happening, I thought. This is crazy!

I wanted to shake him some more, but I was losing strength. My hands went right through him.

Finally, Max let out a groan. He opened one eye. Then, when he saw Tara and me, he sat straight up. "You're still here?" he asked, pulling the sheet up to his chin.

"We . . . we couldn't wake you," I said.

"No one can. I'm a very heavy sleeper," Max said. "Sometimes Mom has to pour ice water on me in the morning to wake me for school."

"You really scared us," Tara told him.

"That's a laugh," Max said. "Me scaring two

ghosts!" He yawned. "I was having the nicest dream. I dreamed you were both *gone*."

"We're not going away," I said. "Not until we find our parents."

"Who is Phears?" Tara asked.

Max blinked. "Who?"

"Phears," Tara repeated. "His name is Phears." She spelled it.

Max shook his head. "Never heard of him. Is he a friend of yours?"

"We need to find him," I said. "We think he's a ghost."

Max let out a cry. "Please—no more ghosts!"

"You've got to help us find Phears," Tara said. "We need someone who is alive. Who won't fade in and out like us." She stuck her hand right through the headboard of Max's bed.

"Will you help us?" I asked.

"No way," Max replied. "Read my lips—*no way*."

I could feel myself fading. I could feel the air blowing through me as if I wasn't there. Tara shimmered weakly. She was disappearing too.

"But we can help you," Tara insisted. "We can help each other. You don't want to go to the Plover School, do you, Max?"

"I'd rather swallow a big hairy rat," he said. "Whole."

"Well, Nicky and I will make sure you don't

have to go there. Promise. We'll make you look awesome and brave. We'll show your dad that you're a total winner."

"Ha!" Max said. "*Me* brave? I'm afraid of my own dog!"

"We promise we'll keep you from the Plover School—if you'll help us find Phears and our parents," Tara said. "Please say yes, Maxie," she whispered. "Please . . ."

Did he agree?

I don't know. I faded away before he gave his answer.

My last thought before I disappeared: We've got to find this guy Phears. He's our only hope.

12

I WOKE UP—WIDE awake. Grabbed the sheet with both hands and gazed around my room.

No ghosts.

Whew.

Were they gone? I hoped so.

I'd had a frightening dream during the night. I dreamed I'd promised to help them find their parents.

Oh no. Wait. I shook myself awake. That wasn't a dream. I really did make a deal with them. But why?

Out of fear, of course.

I was afraid that if I made them angry, they might try to possess me and inhabit my body. Isn't that what ghosts always do? Then you become like a zombie. You lose all control of what you say and do.

Well, I didn't want two ghosts inside my body. It's crowded enough in here already with just me inside.

I glanced around the room. No sign of them.

"Please—disappear forever," I said out loud.

I showered quickly, pulled on a pair of baggy cargo pants and a red and black *Digimon* T-shirt, and hurried down to breakfast.

Still no sign of the two ghosts. That made me very happy. Buster jumped up from under the kitchen table and growled at me.

"Morning, Mom," I said. Dad had already left for work. Colin sat at the breakfast table. I started to sit down, and he pulled my chair out from under me.

"Hey—!" I fell on my butt.

Colin hee-hawed like a donkey.

Mom stood at the stove with her back turned. "I'm making your favorite, Maxie," she said. "Blueberry pancakes."

"Sweet!" I said. Carefully holding on to the chair, I sat down next to Colin. I took a sip from my orange juice glass—and Nicky and Tara popped up on the other side of the table.

"Morning," they said together.

I slapped my forehead. "You're still here?"

"Of course I'm still here," Mom said. "You know I don't go in to work till later."

"We're staying, Max," Tara said. "We're not going away. We made a deal, remember? We're going to stay and help you—so that you can help us."

"But I *can't* help you," I said.

Mom turned from the stove. "You don't need to help me," she said. "The pancakes are all done."

She carried a tall stack of them to the table on a plate.

"Those look good," Nicky said, reaching for the plate.

"Stay away!" I cried.

Mom stared at me. "How can I stay away and bring you your breakfast at the same time?"

"I . . . I wasn't talking to you," I told her.

Colin raised a fist. "You were telling *me* to stay away?"

"No," I said, thinking quickly. I didn't want to get pounded first thing in the morning. "I was talking to myself. I was telling myself to stay away from eating too many pancakes."

Colin lowered his fist.

Why couldn't Mom and Colin see the two ghosts?

Mom poured maple syrup over the blueberry pancakes. Then she crossed the room to get her coffee.

Colin reached for the pancake plate.

But Nicky lifted the stack of pancakes right off the plate. "Yum," he said. "Wish I could share with you guys."

"Put that down!" I shouted.

Colin gasped. He stared at the pancakes—floating in midair. "What is *that*?" he screamed.

"Uh . . . Mom used a very light batter!" I said.

Colin reached up to pull the pancakes down from the air.

Nicky let them drop into Colin's lap.

"Hey—!" Colin bellowed. The sticky syrup oozed over his jeans.

Mom turned around. "Colin, don't play with your food," she said.

"Is this one of your magic tricks, Hamburger?" Colin shouted. "Here's one of mine." He jammed a pancake over my face and smeared it all around.

"Colin!" Mom cried. "What are you doing?"

"Offering Maxie a pancake," he said. He rubbed the syrupy pancake over my hair. Then he jumped up and ran to his room to change into clean pants.

Nicky and Tara reached for his pancakes and began chewing them up. "I thought ghosts can't eat," I whispered.

Nicky shrugged. "No one told us that. We're new at this, you know."

"And we're starving," Tara said. "As soon as we eat, Nicky and I will come to school with you and start helping you."

"No, please," I said, "I don't want to be helped. *Please* don't follow me to school."

Mom stared hard at me. "Max, why would I follow you to school?" she asked.

"Uh . . ." Think quickly, Max. Think quickly. "Uh . . . just in case you missed me?"

She laughed and gave me a hug from behind. "You're a funny kid."

I glared sternly at Nicky and Tara. I wanted to make sure they got the message: I didn't want them to follow me to school. I'm at the top of my class. I don't need help in school.

Think they came to school anyway?

Three guesses.

Think they helped me?

Three guesses.

13

I SAW TRACI WAYNE as I walked to school. Traci is the coolest girl at Jefferson Elementary. I mean, she's the hottest. She's the coolest and the hottest.

Traci is blond and pretty, with olive-colored eyes and a great smile. Actually, I'm not sure about the color of her eyes because I've never stood very close to her. Only the cool kids get to stand close to Traci.

That doesn't mean Traci isn't a nice person. She's very nice and very friendly. But she's so totally awesome and cool that she has no choice—she *has* to hang with cool kids like her.

Traci was the first one in our sixth-grade class to wear purple lipstick. And the first girl to wear a tiny rhinestone stud on one side of her nose. She's just so totally *hot*!

I don't know if I'm in love with Traci or have a crush on her or what. But every time I see her, my cheeks turn bright red, my mouth goes completely dry, and my tongue feels as if it's suddenly too fat to fit in my mouth.

One day last year I tried to say hi to Traci, and all that came out was "Unnngh unnnngh." She thought I was choking and slapped me on the back.

I have this wild daydream that Traci is my assistant for my magic act. I picture her helping me with my Disappearing Girl trick when I perform at the Halloween party at school.

If Traci was my assistant, my act would be the biggest thing in school history. People would see me onstage with her and they might start to think that *I* was cool too!

Sometimes I just shut my eyes and picture what the magic act would be like if Traci was my assistant. Of course, it's a silly daydream. The other kids probably wouldn't think I'm cool, even with Traci. But it's nice to have a daydream, if you're me.

Anyway, I was crossing Powell Avenue, almost to school, when I saw Traci on the corner. I recognized her by her blond hair first. It was fluttering around her head in the wind. She had her backpack down on the ground and was bending over it, searching for something inside it.

I came up behind her. I took a deep breath. "Unnngh unnnngh," I said. That was supposed to be "Yo, what's up?"

She didn't hear me. She didn't look up. She kept searching for something in her backpack.

"Uh . . . hi," I said, but it came out in a dry whisper.

Suddenly, I felt someone beside me. "You like that girl, don't you, Max?" Tara asked.

"What are you doing here?" I cried.

"Searching for my math homework," Traci answered. "Hope I didn't leave it at home."

"You're blushing, Max," Nicky said. "I think you have a crush on that girl."

"Leave me alone," I snapped.

Traci looked up at me. "I'm bothering you?"

"N-no," I stammered. "I just meant—"

Tara said, "Nicky and I are here to help you, Max. Go ahead. Be brave. Bend down and help her search."

"No. Stop," I said.

"Stop *what*?" Traci asked.

"Go ahead, Max. She needs help."

I tried to pull back. But Tara gave me a hard push. I stumbled—*and fell on top of Traci*!

Traci let out a startled cry. My stomach landed on top of her head. We both toppled onto her backpack. "You're *crushing* me!" she shrieked.

I thrashed my arms wildly in the air, struggling to stand up. Finally, Traci shoved me with both hands and I dropped, sitting down, onto the sidewalk.

The papers from her backpack were strewn all over the grass. Her hair was matted against her head. She turned to me and laughed. "Are you on the football team?"

"No," I choked out.

"You should be. That was a great tackle."

"Sorry." I could feel my face turn hot. I knew I must be as red as the stoplight over the street.

"Go ahead," Tara said, standing over me. "Be brave. Tell her you think she's hot."

"No way," I said.

"No way *what*?" Traci asked. She stuffed her papers back into the backpack.

"I wasn't talking to you," I said.

She glanced around. "Max, who were you talking to?"

"Uh . . . myself."

Traci narrowed her eyes at me. "You're weird."

"Yeah, I know," I muttered.

"Ask her to play tennis with you after school," Tara said.

"It's too cold for tennis," I said.

Traci looked confused. "What about tennis?"

"I don't play it," I said.

She tossed her backpack over her shoulder. "Then why are you talking about it? Never mind. We're going to be late." She turned and started to jog away.

"Traci? Would you like to help me with my magic act?" I called after her.

She didn't hear me. She just kept running down the sidewalk.

I rolled my eyes. "Thanks for your help," I muttered to Nicky and Tara.

But of course the two troublemakers had disappeared.

I ran into Ms. McDonald's classroom just as the bell rang. I spotted Traci, already in her seat in the front row. I could feel my face growing hot again.

She didn't see me. She was talking to one of her cool friends, Monica Wendt, who sat beside her.

I knew Traci would never speak to me again.

Can you imagine the horror of having a crush on a girl and then *falling on top of her*? Of course it wasn't my fault. But could I explain to Traci that a ghost named Tara had shoved me into her?

Yeah, sure.

I slunk to my seat in the back. I had grass stains on the knees of my cargo pants. And in my rush to get out of the house and away from the ghosts, I'd forgotten to bring my backpack with all my homework in it.

I froze in panic. I didn't have my homework—*for the first time in my life*!

At the chalkboard, Ms. McDonald was busy

writing an endless algebra equation. Algebra is one of my best subjects. I can solve any equation forward and backward.

Ms. McDonald turned to the class. She's a nice teacher, very young and very pretty. She has curly black hair down past her shoulders, and bright blue eyes. She always wears faded jeans and bright-colored sweaters.

She also has a good sense of humor. Sometimes kids call her Ms. Mickey D, and she doesn't mind it at all.

"Who can solve this equation?" she asked, her eyes shifting from face to face.

I raised my hand.

"I know *you* can do it, Max," Ms. McDonald said. "Does anyone else want to try?"

No hands went up. "Okay, Max. Come up and show us how to solve it," Ms. McDonald said.

I walked to the front of the room. I was careful not to look at Traci. "Go, Brainimon!" a boy yelled from the back. A few kids laughed.

"Make it hard. Do it blindfolded," Monica Wendt called out.

"Brainimon can do it!" another boy shouted.

I felt good. This was the only time in school I felt like a real winner. I took the chalk from Ms. McDonald and turned to the board. I started to factor for X, writing quickly, the chalk squeaking in my hand.

"Hey, I know how to do this one," I heard Nicky say. "Give me the chalk."

"No. Go away!" I said.

Ms. McDonald took a few steps back. "Sorry, Max. Was I standing in your light?"

"You're messing up. You should do the fractions first," Nicky said. "Give me the chalk. I'll show you." I felt him grab my hand. He tried to pull the chalk away. I struggled to hold on, and we battled for it.

Some kids started to laugh.

"What's wrong, Max? Do you have a cramp?" Ms. McDonald asked.

Nicky wrapped his hand around mine. "Let me help you, Max. I'm an ace at this." He forced me to write a string of numbers on the board.

"Stop! Don't help me!" I cried.

"I won't help you," Ms. McDonald said. "I know you never need help, Max."

"Let go of me," I whispered to Nicky. But he gripped my hand and wrote out more letters and numbers.

"Am I getting it right?" he asked Tara.

"How should I know?" Tara answered. "I'm only in fourth grade. I never had algebra."

"Go away," I whispered. My hand was writing out of control. Nicky wouldn't stop—and he was getting it totally wrong!

I turned and saw Mrs. Wright, the principal,

enter the room. She and Ms. McDonald began talking at the side of the chalkboard.

"Do you know how to do this?" Nicky asked Tara.

Tara tugged at her floppy red hat with both hands. "No way."

"I think I messed up," Nicky said. He moved my hand and forced me to erase half the equation.

Kids were mumbling to themselves in shock. They knew I'd never messed up an equation in my life.

"Now what?" Nicky said to Tara.

"Why are you asking *me*?" Tara snapped.

I couldn't take it anymore. *"Shut up!"* I screamed. *"Both of you—shut up!"*

Ms. McDonald and Mrs. Wright both gasped.

"Max—I am shocked at you. That's no way to talk to the principal and me!" Ms. McDonald exclaimed.

Mrs. Wright glared at me angrily. "Max, you and I need to have a long talk about politeness. I'll see you right now. In my office."

14

MRS. WRIGHT AND I had a *very* long talk about politeness. Only, she did all the talking. I didn't get out of her office until lunchtime.

Kids were laughing and shouting in the halls. Lockers slammed. The line was already a mile long in the lunchroom. I looked for Aaron, but I couldn't find him.

"Hey, Max—shut up!" a kid from my class named Wilson Grant shouted across the hall at me. A bunch of kids laughed.

"Yeah, shut up, Brainimon!" another kid echoed. They all laughed again.

So, I was the joke of the day. The Shut Up Kid. Ha, ha. Remind me to laugh someday.

I picked up a tray in the lunchroom and chose a bowl of the tomato soup and a slice of pizza, and a carton of chocolate milk. I was paying for my lunch when Nicky and Tara appeared.

"Sorry about this morning," Nicky said. "I thought I knew how to do that equation." He

scratched his spikey brown hair. “Maybe I knew it when I was alive.”

“Go away,” I said, looking for an empty chair. “You got me into major trouble. Let me eat my lunch—alone.”

“There’s your girlfriend,” Tara said. She pointed to Traci, seated at the cool kids’ table on the side.

“She’s not my girlfriend,” I said. “Please—go away.”

“Go talk to her,” Tara said. “There’s an empty seat across from her.”

“I can’t sit there. That’s the cool kids’ table,” I said.

Some kids turned to stare at me. I’m sure they wondered why I was standing in the middle of the lunchroom talking to myself.

“You know you want to talk to Traci,” Nicky said. “Come on. You’ve got to be brave, Max—if you’re ever going to help us find our mom and dad.”

“Let go of me!” I shouted.

More kids turned to stare.

Nicky and Tara grabbed me under the arms and moved me toward Traci’s table. I gripped the tray tightly in both hands. I tried to pull free.

Despite my struggle to get loose, the two ghosts carried me all the way to Traci. They let go without warning. I lost my balance and tumbled forward. The tray flew from my hands—and sailed upside down onto Traci.

Traci's hands flew up and she let out a scream as the tomato soup poured down the front of her T-shirt and vest. The pizza slice landed in her lap.

Kids gasped. The other kids at Traci's table leaped away.

I stared at her as she pulled the pizza off her legs. Long strands of cheese stuck to her jeans.

My whole body was trembling. I took a deep breath. I figured I didn't have anything to lose. "Traci, will you be my assistant in my magic show?" I blurted out.

Her mouth dropped open. She squinted at me. "Okay, fine," she said, tugging cheese from her jeans. "If you promise *never* to come near me again."

"Awesome!" I said. I staggered away. Was I hearing right? Did she really say yes?

"See?" Tara said, back at my side, a big grin under the red flap of her hat. "Nicky and I are improving your life already!"

"Shut up!" I cried.

I didn't see Mrs. Wright standing beside me. She shook her head angrily. "Max, I guess we didn't have a long enough chat this morning. See you in my office after school. And maybe we should have your parents in too."

15

AS I SLUNK DOWN the long hall to the principal's office, Nicky and Tara appeared beside me. "Go away," I said through clenched teeth.

"We're sorry," Nicky said. "We only tried to help."

"Yes, we're sorry. We'll do a better job this afternoon," Tara said. "You'll see."

"No, I won't see," I said. Two kids from my class turned to see who I was talking to. "Go home," I told the two ghosts. "Everyone is staring at me. Please—wait for me in my room. Don't go anywhere. I mean it. Wait for me there. We have to have a long talk."

They both had hurt expressions on their faces. "You don't want us to help you in gym class?" Nicky asked.

"Just wait for me in my room," I snapped. I spun away and strode into the principal's office for my second lecture of the day.

• • •

By the time Mrs. Wright let me go home, the sun was setting. A cold October wind whistled down from the hills above school.

I zipped up my purple and gray Jefferson Middle School jacket, a hand-me-down from Colin. And hunching into the wind, I started to climb the hill toward home.

I really am hamburger meat now, I thought bitterly. When Mom and Dad find out they have to come to school for a talk with the principal, I'm totally busted.

They might even ground me for Halloween. I won't get to perform my magic act, which I've been practicing day and night for at least a year. And I won't have Traci as my assistant.

And then they'll send me to the Plover School, where I'll have to wear an ugly starched uniform and do sit-ups every morning till I barf.

And is it my fault?

No way.

Can I help it if I'm being haunted by two stupid ghosts?

A shiver ran down my body. From the wind? Or from knowing that I was being haunted by two dead kids? Two dead kids who followed me everywhere and wouldn't leave me alone. Two dead kids who wanted me to help them.

I didn't want to help them. I didn't want to be haunted.

Why was I the only one who could see and hear them? How could I be so unlucky?

How could I get rid of them?

A red SUV rumbled past. The back window rolled down. A kid stuck out his head and shouted, "Shut up! Shut up!" Laughing, he rolled up the window.

That's me. Mr. Shut Up.

The bare trees rattled over my head. The ground was crunchy from an early frost.

Almost Halloween, I thought. My favorite holiday. But . . . it won't be any fun for me this year.

I didn't see the squirrel until I turned onto Bleek Street.

It was a scrawny brown squirrel, and it seemed to be following me. It gazed up at me with its black eyes, twitching its nose as it kept in step with me.

I stopped and waved both hands in a shooing motion. "Scat. Get lost!" I shouted.

To my surprise, the squirrel hopped even closer. It stood right at my feet.

"Go away! Get lost!"

But the squirrel wasn't afraid of me. It stood its ground.

And then the squirrel's jaws opened wide. I stared in amazement as a sticky black goo came spewing out of its mouth—*onto my shoes*. I tried to jump back. But the goo was as thick as tar and held me in place.

The squirrel spewed up more black tar, covering my feet completely. And then, to my horror, the little animal exploded. It blew apart—fur and bones and squirrel guts flying all around me. The two little eyeballs bounced and rolled down the hill.

I felt sick. I doubled over and grabbed my churning stomach—and saw a big blob of the black goo at my feet begin to move. It floated up and dissolved into a heavy gray fog.

And in the fog, I saw a ghostly figure—a man in a long black cloak. He moved forward quickly, a black shadow against the billowing gray mist.

"Remember me, Max?" he shouted in a booming voice that made the trees rattle even harder.

Huh? I was too terrified to speak. I just stood there gaping up at him.

"Of course you don't remember me. I clouded your memory," he said, floating closer. "Well, let me give you a little reminder of what I can do. Ever go to the dentist, Max? Ever had all your teeth drilled at once?"

"Who are you?" I shrieked. I tried to run, but the black goo over my shoes held me in place. "Leave me alone!"

He smiled an ugly smile. Then, with a wave of his hand, the pain began.

It felt like dentist drills, whirring and whistling, digging deep, digging into all my teeth at once.

"*Ow!* Please—stop! Oh no! It hurts! It hurts! Stop!"

16

MY HEAD EXPLODED IN pain.

No way to escape it . . . the hot, sharp drilling . . . *in all my teeth*! The horrifying sound rose like a shrill siren. Steam poured from my open mouth.

"Ohhhhh." I shut my eyes and grabbed the sides of my face.

"Stop—please!" The raging pain seared through my head, into my *brain*. I could feel my face swell up like a balloon. I opened my mouth to scream, but the whistle of the invisible drills drowned out all sound.

I fell to the ground, pulled free of the black goo, and began rolling in the grass, still holding the sides of my face.

Finally, the drilling stopped.

The sudden silence seemed so *loud*.

My face pounded and ached. I tried to blink away the dizziness.

"Now let me introduce myself," the ghostly figure's voice boomed from inside his dark storm cloud. "My name is Phears, and I am the Animal-Traveler."

I buried my face under my arms, wishing him away, wishing the pain would stop.

"Where are they?" Phears demanded, hovering over me. "I know they are with you. Don't lie to me."

I kept my face covered and my eyes shut. My mind whirred. *Phears*. He said his name is Phears. He's the guy Nicky and Tara are looking for.

And he must be looking for them.

But he's terrifying. He's totally evil. Should I tell him Nicky and Tara are looking for him? Should I tell him they're in my room?

"I . . . I . . ." My voice came out in a faint whisper. I opened my eyes and peeked up at him through my hands. I couldn't see his face. It was covered in swirls of fog. But I could see two pale eyes glowing angrily at me.

My ears still whistled from the roar of the drills. I slid my tongue back and forth over my teeth. Were they full of holes?

"I must see Nicky and Tara Roland," Phears said. "Can you help me find them, Max? I only want to *talk* with them."

"I . . . I . . ."

"Stop stammering, Max!" Phears boomed. "I'm tired of playing nice with you."

Playing *nice*?

"You know where they are!" Phears shouted. "Tell me where they're hiding."

Should I tell him?

No. He didn't want to help them. He wanted to hurt them. I knew it.

"No," I said. "I . . . can't help you. I . . ."

"Let me help you remember," Phears said. He raised a shadowy hand. The shrill siren whirred to life inside my head. The drills bore down again.

My mouth shot open in pain. Gobs of saliva poured down my chin.

Choking, I buried my head in my hands. I tried to hold my head together. But I knew it was about to explode—just like that poor squirrel!

"Okay. Okay!" I screamed, holding my head. "I know them! I know where they are! Please—make it stop!"

Everything went bright red, then black. I may have fainted. I'm not sure. When I opened my eyes, my mouth ached but the drilling had stopped.

Phears hovered over me, floating in his dark storm cloud. "Now we're getting somewhere. Where are they hiding?"

He raised his hand, ready to start the drills again.

"No. Please—" I said. "They're looking for you. They're in my bedroom right now."

"Liar!" Phears cried. "I've already searched

your bedroom. I didn't find any sign of them." He raised his hand menacingly.

"Sometimes they're invisible. But they're both in my bedroom right now!" I screamed. "They want to see you. I promise. You'll find them there."

Phears stared at me for a long moment. "They want to see me? How bizarre." He turned away quickly. Then his body melted into a heavy gray mist.

I saw a brown and black chipmunk scampering down the hill toward me. It darted one way, then the other as it came near. It ran right into the mist. And with a loud *whooooosh,* the gray fog shot into the little creature's mouth as if the chipmunk was drinking up the fog.

I climbed slowly to my feet. I watched the chipmunk's whole body shudder. I knew Phears was inside it now. And I knew where he was heading.

To my house. To my bedroom.

The two ghosts would soon be gone. My life would return to normal.

Did I feel good about it?

Not exactly. I felt like a rat.

I clicked my teeth together. They seemed to be okay. But just *remembering* the pain of those invisible drills made my stomach tighten and my heart start to pound.

I had no choice. Phears was going to destroy me. I *had* to tell him where Nicky and Tara were hiding. Besides, they couldn't wait to see Phears. Maybe I helped them after all. Maybe I did a *good* thing. Maybe . . .

I took my time getting home. I walked as slowly as I could. I didn't want Phears to still be there when I arrived.

One of our neighbors had raked his leaves down to the street. I walked slowly through the pile, kicking up leaves as I walked.

Then I stopped to wave to Edgar. The Swansons' black cat sat on his usual perch in their front window. I waved and called his name. I think he was glad to see me. It's hard to tell with cats.

Finally, I let myself into the house through the kitchen door. "Anyone home?" I called.

No reply.

Too early for Mom and Dad to be home. Colin was probably at school practicing with the basketball team.

I made my way to the stairs. "Anyone up there?" I called, cupping my hands around my mouth.

Again, no answer.

I climbed the stairs slowly. My legs felt a little shaky, and my mouth suddenly got dry. "Hey—anyone?" I shouted.

I stepped into my room—and let out a horrified cry.

What a mess!

The whole room had been trashed! Turned upside down!

My bedcovers were balled up on the floor. My mattress stood on its side. All my clothes had been pulled from the closet and strewn over the room. The dresser drawers had all been heaved out and emptied, everything dumped in the middle of the floor.

"Oh no. Oh no. Oh no." I shook my head over and over. "Oh no. Oh no." I couldn't stop saying it.

And there . . . there on my desk . . .

"Oh no. Oh no."

I squinted hard at it until it came into focus. Tara's red hat. The floppy red hat she never took off.

There it stood, ripped in half on my desk.

"Oh no. Oh no," I moaned. "Nicky? Tara? *What have I done?*"

17

WHAT DID PHEARS DO to them?

I picked up the torn red hat and moved it around in my hands. A sob escaped my throat.

Phears must have done something horrible to them, and it was all my fault.

I tossed Tara's hat aside, and then I dropped onto the pile of clothes on my floor. I buried my face in my hands.

They wanted to be my friends. They were all alone and totally confused, and they needed me to help them.

They thought they were safe with me. And what did I do?

I gave away their hiding place. Phears probably tortured them. Then he made them disappear forever. And now they'll never find their parents.

Did I ever feel more miserable in my life?

I don't think so.

I felt so bad, I was shaking. I hugged myself to try to stop it. I could barely breathe.

I made a silent promise to myself. If the two

ghosts somehow escaped Phears, I would help them. I would stop fighting with them and try to help them find their parents.

And then I felt a tap on my shoulder.

Startled, I jumped. And stared up at Nicky and Tara. I blinked several times. Was I seeing things?

"You missed all the excitement," Nicky said.

"We were so scared," Tara said. "We thought Phears could help us. We wanted to talk to him. But as soon as he saw us, he started screaming about Mom and Dad."

"He's crazy," Nicky said. "He kept asking us, 'Where are they? Where are they hiding?' We told him we didn't know. But he didn't believe us."

Tara's chin trembled. "It was so horrible. Phears made a grab for me. I ducked, and he got my hat. Then Nicky and I went invisible. Phears was so angry, he ripped the hat in two. Then he trashed the room. He just went berserk."

My heart pounding, I jumped to my feet. "But—but you're both okay?"

"I guess," Tara said. "It was really frightening."

I was so happy to see them, I hugged them both.

Nicky stared at me in surprise. "Max, you're starting to *like* us?"

"I . . . was worried about you," I said. "I saw Tara's hat and . . ."

Nicky scratched his head. "Who *is* this guy Phears? What is his *problem*?"

"Lulu said he knows about Mom and Dad," Tara said. Her chin trembled again. "I . . . hope he hasn't done something bad to them."

I squinted at her. "Lulu? Who is Lulu?"

"Our old nanny," Tara said. "We saw her in the kitchen. She's a ghost too."

So *that's* who I heard late at night, I realized. I knew it. I knew our house was already haunted!

Nicky started to pace back and forth. "Phears was our only clue to finding Mom and Dad. But we can't talk to him. He's evil. Maybe Lulu was trying to *warn* us about Phears."

Tara turned to me. "Whoa. Wait a minute. How did Phears know where to find us?"

I swallowed. "Well . . . "

I could feel my face turning red. I suddenly felt sick. I didn't want to tell them I was the one who ratted on them. Now that I realized they were my friends, I didn't want them to hate me.

"Max—!"

A cry from the doorway saved me from having to answer. I turned to see Mom standing there, her eyes wide with horror. Her mouth kept opening and closing as she stared at the total mess, but it took her a long time to speak.

"Max—this mess! You—you—you—"

Think fast, Max. Think fast. "It's all an optical illusion, Mom," I said.

"Excuse me?"

"Yes, it's part of my magic act for the Halloween party. I'll make the mess totally disappear before supper."

Mom stared hard at me. "You'd better make it disappear, Max. Your dad is *not* going to be in a good mood when he gets home from work. We got a call from the principal. She said you were very rude to her."

"It's all a big mistake," I said. I turned to Nicky and Tara, but they had disappeared.

Mom frowned at me. "I always taught you good manners, didn't I, Maxie? Did you really tell Mrs. Wright to shut up?"

"No. No way," I said. "She didn't hear me right. I said *thumbs* up. Yeah. That's what I said. *Thumbs* up. I was being cheerful, see? Showing her some good attitude."

Did Mom believe me? I couldn't tell. "Get this mess cleaned up, Max," she said. "Fast. And you can stop rehearsing your magic act. You're going to be grounded for Halloween."

"No—!" I screamed. "You *can't*!"

But she was already on her way down the stairs.

"No! No way! What am I supposed to do with my bear costume? I promised Aaron we'd go trick-or-treating. And what about my magic act?"

Nicky and Tara appeared beside me. "Take it easy, Max," Nicky said. "We'll help you clean your room up."

"No!" I screamed. *"I can't be grounded! I can't!"*

Furious, I picked up my backpack—and heaved it across the room. It hit the wall hard. I heard a loud *crack*. And to my shock, a wall panel fell off. It broke off the wall and toppled to the floor.

"Huh—?" I could see a square of darkness behind the wall. An opening.

Nicky, Tara, and I crossed the room and stared into the hole.

"Just like Lulu said," Tara murmured. "A tunnel."

18

STARING INTO THE DARK hole, I felt a chill. The air on the other side of the wall felt cold and damp.

I took a few steps back, into the warmth of my room. "How can there be a tunnel up here?" I asked. "We're upstairs. And you can't see any tunnel from outside the house."

The two ghosts stared silently into the black tunnel opening.

"This is so exciting!" Tara exclaimed. She slapped Nicky a high five. "Lulu said that Mom and Dad discovered a tunnel. This must be it."

"Wow! Maybe it will lead us to Mom and Dad," Nicky said.

I could tell they were excited. They kept fading away, then reappearing brightly, flickering at the tunnel opening like fireflies.

"Are you going in there?" I asked.

"We can't. Lulu said we can't go in the tunnel," Tara answered. "She said if we went in, we'd never return."

"But we have to find out what's in there,"

Nicky said. "We have to find out if it leads to Mom and Dad."

"Then who's going to go?" I asked.

They both turned to me. "Max—?"

"Whoa. Time out," I said, doing a football time-out signal. "No way I'm going in that tunnel. I'm allergic to tunnels. My whole face breaks out. Really."

Tara floated over to me. Without the hat covering her face, she was kinda cute. She had wavy brown hair and sparkling green eyes. I really hadn't noticed before.

"We need your help," she said softly. "Phears will come back looking for us, you know."

"And he'll come back for you, too, Max," Nicky said.

I swallowed. My teeth began to hurt again, just thinking about Phears.

They turned to me. "We have to find Mom and Dad before Phears does," Tara said.

"I . . . can't go in there," I said. "I'd like to help you. Really. But you heard my mom. I have to clean up my room."

Tara slid her arm around my shoulders in kind of a hug. "We'll clean your room for you, Maxie," she said softly.

I never had a girl put her arm around me before. The back of my neck tingled.

What a shame that the first girl to hug me had to be dead!

"We'll clean your room, and we'll guard the tunnel opening," Nicky said. "We'll watch out for you."

I stared at the hole in my bedroom wall. Tara still had her arm around my shoulders. She played with the silver bullet pendant that dangled down to my chest.

"Maybe the tunnel is very short," I said.

"Good attitude," Tara said.

"But what do I look for?" I asked. "How do I search for something if I don't know what it is?"

Nicky shrugged. "Look for our mom and dad," he said.

"Or any kind of clue about us or them," Tara said. "Anything!"

I rolled my eyes. "Oh, good. That makes it easy."

I walked over to the tunnel opening and peered in again. A whiff of cold air greeted me. It smelled sour and musty.

I shivered. "I can't do this," I said. "I'm sorry. I want to help you out. But this is too scary."

Tara handed me a flashlight. "Hurry, Max. Phears will be back. He'll do horrible things to us."

I ran my tongue over my teeth. Once again, I remembered the pain of the invisible dentist drills.

"Maybe it will be easy," Nicky said. "Maybe you'll find it right away."

"Whatever it is," I muttered.

I took a step into the tunnel. Then another.

Darkness surrounded me right away like a heavy blanket wrapping around me. The clammy air chilled my skin.

I took another step—and heard a scraping sound behind me.

"Huh—?" I wheeled around—in time to see the tunnel opening slide shut.

I hurried back toward my room. And slapped out with both hands.

Solid wall. The opening had closed.

I was trapped on the other side.

19

MY HEART STARTED TO race. I pounded on the wall with both fists.

"Hey—can anybody hear me in there? Nicky? Tara? Help me!"

I pressed my ear to the wall and listened. The wall felt cold and damp against my skin. I couldn't hear anyone on the other side.

I picked up the flashlight and pounded it hard against the wall. "Open up in there! Somebody—help me! I'm trapped in here!"

Silence.

I pounded some more, then waited. But I knew the wall wasn't going to slide open again.

Gripping the flashlight, I turned toward the darkness.

"I'm not brave," I said out loud. "So what am I doing here?" My voice echoed as if I was in a huge cave.

Where *am* I? I wondered. How can there be a tunnel inside my house? Did Nicky and Tara's parents disappear into this tunnel? I wanted

to shut off my brain, but the questions wouldn't stop.

And then I heard a crackling sound, far in the distance but growing louder. I heard the whoosh of air. Flapping.

Flapping wings?

Yes. I raised the beam of light from the flashlight—and saw the flying creatures. Bats, black against the black tunnel ceiling. Thousands of tiny red eyes darted over me like insects. In seconds, the sound of the flapping wings grew to a roar.

"*Nooooo—!*" I let out a horrified cry and covered my head with my arms.

I could feel bursts of wind as their wings beat against my face. Something brushed the top of my head, and I screamed again.

Covering my head, I swung away from them. A bat flew hard into the back of my neck. I felt its dry, hot body on my skin, then felt the scratch of a talon and a sharp stab of pain.

The roar of their beating wings surrounded me, so loud I couldn't think. Another bat grazed the back of my head. A bat hit my neck and slid down the back of my T-shirt.

"Ohhhhhh." I uttered a terrified moan as I felt its crackly, dry body slide down my back. I twitched and thrashed, slapping at the back of my shirt—until the creature fell out, dropped to the tunnel floor, then flew away.

My breath came out in short gasps. The bats pounded against me. I tried to fold myself into a tight ball, but I couldn't get small enough to escape them.

Finally, I stood up straight. I swung toward them and waved the light back and forth wildly. Their silky wings caught the light. Their flight slowed.

The bats began to screech, a high whistle that made my ears ring. Frantically, I shot the light back and forth like a light saber in *Star Wars*.

To my shock, the attack stopped. The bats floated high above me now, avoiding the light. "Die! Die! Die!" I screamed, enjoying my new power. I aimed the light beam and watched the bats flee.

Silence now, except for the wheezing of my own breath. I bent over, lowered my hands to the knees of my jeans, and waited for my breathing to return to normal.

Did those bats attack me for a reason? I wondered. Were they trying to keep me away from something?

I rubbed the back of my neck. I had a few scratches back there, but nothing serious.

Aiming the circle of light on the tunnel floor, I started walking. My legs still felt shaky. Despite the cool air, sweat poured down my forehead.

I walked slowly, my sneakers shuffling along the slick, hard tunnel floor.

I kept walking, sweeping the light from side to side on the floor. Something sticky brushed my face. Cobwebs?

The thick web tightened around me like a mask. I raised my free hand and tried to tug it away. But it stuck to my hand and began to wrap itself around my wrist.

It's alive, I realized. A throbbing, breathing cobweb!

I dropped the flashlight and ripped the sticky, pulsing strings off my face with both hands. Then I tugged the tangled webbing off my arm. I heaved it to the ground and began to stomp on it.

But it stuck to my sneakers and began to creep up around my ankles.

"No—!" I let out a scream as it throbbed against my skin and began to pull me to the floor. I dropped to my knees and pounded it with the head of the flashlight.

But the cobweb stuck to the flashlight and began to spread over it, too. The webbing wrapped around my hand, then my arm. Thick strings of cobweb creeping up, reaching . . . reaching for my neck.

I'm being sucked into it, I realized. It's going to cover me like a cocoon. I'm going to suffocate....

Then to my shock, it all fell away. The webbing let go, lost its stickiness.

As I gazed in amazement, it fell to the floor—and shrank until nothing was left of it.

I jumped to my feet. My skin tingled and itched. Sweat poured down my face and made my T-shirt cling to my back.

Why had the cobweb given up? Why did it draw back just when it had me in its grip?

I turned and saw the reason.

Squinting into the darkness, I saw the ghost coming for me.

My scream rang off the tunnel walls and echoed into the deep chamber.

The ghost floated in the distance, a silent, gray figure against the blackness.

Should I run?

Before I could move, the ghost roared up to me like a tiny, dark tornado. It floated in front of me with its back turned.

The frozen air swirled around me. I fell back against the tunnel wall. "Who are you?" My question came out in a trembling whisper. "What do you want?"

Floating above the floor, it didn't turn around.

Unable to stop my trembling, I stared hard at it. Stared hard . . .

And then it turned around—and I couldn't keep my shock inside. My mouth shot open in a scream of horror.

The ghost had my *face!*

20

THE GHOST STARED AT me blankly, ignoring my scream of horror.

"Are you—?" I started. "Who . . . are you? Are you *me*?"

The ghost gazed back wide-eyed and didn't reply.

I stared at him, stared into my own face. He wore a long white T-shirt, loose-fitting, long as a dress. Beneath it he had on baggy white pants that came down over his shoes.

His eyes were deep set and sad, dark in his pale bleached face. His cheeks were hard and white as cement. His lips were colorless. He studied me as I studied him.

"Can you help me?" I asked. "Where am I? What are you doing here? Are you my ghost? Can you speak?" My questions came out high and frightened.

He floated closer. "Trade places with me," he whispered.

"Excuse me?" I took a step back.

"Trade places with me," he repeated. And then his face began to change. And I was no longer staring at myself. I was staring at a white-haired old man.

"Trade places with me," he rasped.

"No—!" I cried. I took another stumbling step back.

And his face changed again—into that of a sunken-eyed young man. His nose was missing. I stared at the hole in his face. And when he opened his mouth, I saw that he had no teeth and his gums were ripped and jagged.

"Trade places with me."

"No. Stop. I won't," I said. Then I noticed that he had something half hidden in his hand. As I squinted at it, he held it up so that I could see it better.

"I have what you're looking for," he croaked.

A shoe box. A cardboard shoe box. And on the side I could see words printed in black marker: N ROLAND.

Nicky Roland. A shoe box belonging to Nicky.

"Oh, wow." I reached out for the shoe box.

The ghost lowered the box to his side. "Trade places with me."

"No. I can't. I don't want to. I'm alive. I'm not a ghost," I said.

"Trade places with me," he repeated. He changed again, into a beefy-faced man with a patch over one eye and ratty black hair flowing down to his shoulders.

He floated higher off the floor. I saw him tighten his free hand into a fist. *"Trade places with me!"* he screamed. His single dark eye flamed, then glowed bright red.

I tried to back away, but I was already pressed against the tunnel wall.

With a furious cry, he shot his fist forward.

I ducked under it. Then I reached up—and grabbed the shoe box from his other hand.

He swiped at the box. Missed.

I darted under him. Wrapping the box in my arms, I started to run. My sneakers slapped the hard floor. Protecting the box, I kept my head low and ran full speed back toward my room.

I glanced back and saw him floating in place, watching me escape. "Trade places with me!" he called.

I turned and ran. The solid black wall stood up ahead. Still no opening back to my room.

Gripping the box, I stopped running. Panting hard, I stood and stared at the wall. I had Nicky's box. But now I seemed to be stuck here. No escape from the tunnel.

With a groan, I sank to the floor. I sat down cross-legged with the box between my knees.

"Hey—!" I cried out when I felt the pull. A strong force, pulling me *into* the black wall.

I grabbed the shoe box. I tried to stand up. But the force was too powerful. I felt like a tiny tack being pulled by a powerful magnet.

Phears!

The thought of his name sent a shiver down my back.

Somehow Phears had followed me. And now he was pulling me toward him, pulling me into the wall.

The force tugged me by the feet. I struggled to stand up, but it was too powerful. I couldn't fight it.

Flat on my back, gripping the box in both hands, I slid feetfirst toward the opening. Desperate to pull free, I dug my sneakers into the floor. I twisted my body and shoved one hand onto the floor.

Gripping the floor, digging in my heels, I slowed my slide. But the force was too powerful to resist.

I heard a *thud*. Felt a crushing blow at the back of my head.

I remember the pain. I remember collapsing lifelessly to the tunnel floor. I remember the blackness sweeping over me.

That's all I remember.

21

I CAME BACK TO life slowly, blinking, my head aching. I struggled to focus my eyes.

Where was I?

The back of my head throbbed with pain. Lying flat on my back, I squinted across the room. I saw a dresser with a lamp on it, a Lara Croft poster on the wall behind it.

I sat up with a groan. I slapped the mattress with both hands. I was in my own bed, in my bedroom. Or was this some kind of trick? Had Phears pulled me into a parallel universe? (I saw an episode of *Outer Limits* that was like that.)

Leaning on my elbows, I pulled myself up higher.

"Awesome. Check out Sleeping Beauty," a girl's voice said. Tara popped into view beside the bed.

"Our hero," Nicky declared. He appeared on the other side of the bed.

I blinked again. "Am I really home?"

"Yeah, thanks to us," Nicky said. "We pulled

you out of the tunnel. But it took all our strength away. After we got you in bed, we vaporized for hours."

"Why did you fight us like that?" Tara demanded. "We were trying to save your life. We were trying to pull you to safety, and you gave us such a hard time. What was up with that?"

"I had to hit you on the head to make you stop battling us," Nicky said.

"I . . . I thought you were Phears," I said. "I'm sorry, guys."

"No problem," Nicky said. He held up the shoe box and grinned at me. "You the man, Max. You the man!"

I climbed out of bed, grinning. "Yes. I found that box."

"I knew you were secretly brave," Tara said.

"Am I?" I asked weakly.

Nicky slapped me a high five. "You the man!" he repeated. "This is so awesome! I know the box belongs to me, but I can't remember what's in it. Maybe it has some clues about Mom and Dad—or how we ended up as ghosts."

"You didn't open it?" I asked.

"We were too weak," Nicky said. "Besides, we wanted to wait for you. Let's open it now." He pulled off the lid and dumped the contents onto my bed.

"Wow! Look at all this stuff!" Nicky exclaimed.

"Hey—I'm starting to remember some of it. It's a bunch of junk I collected."

I leaned forward to examine the contents of the box. I saw a small square mirror, two comic books, a sealed glass bottle that appeared to be empty, a red plastic ball, a wristwatch with a totally blank face, a framed photograph, a glowing red ring . . .

"Wow! Check out that ring!" I said. I picked it up and studied it. "What makes it glow like that?"

Nicky frowned at it. "I don't know. I don't remember that ring at all."

"It looks like a real magician's ring," I said. "Can I wear it on Halloween when I do my magic act?"

"No problem," Nicky said. "But aren't you grounded for Halloween?"

"Mom will probably let me go," I said. "Especially when she sees how neat my room is. Good job, guys."

Nicky scratched his head and stared down at all the stuff. "I hid this box away for a reason," he said. "But I can't remember why. And how did it end up in that tunnel?"

Tara picked up the framed photograph, and her eyes grew wide. "Oh, wow. Look, Nicky. It's Mom and Dad."

They gazed at the photo with sad smiles. "They look so young in this picture," Nicky said.

He turned the frame so I could see it. I saw a young couple, both with wavy dark hair, standing on an ocean beach. The man was very tanned and had bright blue eyes. He had his arm around his wife, who was thin and much shorter than him, and had an awesome smile.

"They look really nice," I said. I could see that Nicky and Tara were near tears.

"We've got to find them," Tara whispered. "What if they're in trouble?"

Nicky gripped the photo tightly in his hands and studied it. "I'm starting to remember things," he said. "It's like the photo is giving off clues."

"What do you remember?" Tara asked.

"Mom and Dad were scientists. Yes. I can see them wearing white lab coats. They were scientists . . . and they studied . . . they studied . . . ghosts! Yes. I remember. Ghosts!"

"Ghosts?" I said. "For real?"

He nodded. "Paranormal activities. The supernatural."

"Cool," I said. "That's amazing."

"I remember now . . . ," Nicky said, gripping the photo tightly. "They thought they could capture ghosts. No, wait. Maybe they *did* capture ghosts."

"Did they capture them in that tunnel?" I asked.

Nicky shut his eyes and squeezed the photo

frame in his hands. "That's all the photo is telling me. I can't get any more from it."

"Let me hold it," Tara said. She grabbed the photo from Nicky and raised it close to her face.

I heard thudding footsteps. "Hey, Maxie—what's up?" Colin burst into the room. He took a few steps, then froze. His mouth dropped open. "Hey—that picture! It's floating in mid-air!"

I grabbed it away from Tara. "Oh . . . uh . . . yeah," I said, thinking quickly. "Someone sent it to me airmail."

Colin stared at it in my hands. "Weird."

"What do you want, Colin?" I asked.

He pointed to the Halloween costume I had draped over my desk chair. The big furry bear costume I planned to wear for trick-or-treating.

"Maxie, remember I said you could come trick-or-treating with my friends?"

"Yeah, I remember," I said. "Mom said I couldn't go trick-or-treating with just Aaron. I had to go with some bigger kids."

"Well, you can't come with me and my friends," Colin said. "Because that stupid bear costume is too dorky. We'd be embarrassed to be seen with you."

"But . . . but . . . ," I sputtered. "*You* picked it out for me!"

Colin shrugged. "Too bad. Your costume sucks big-time."

"But that means I can't go trick-or-treating!" I cried.

Colin laughed his nastiest laugh. "Tough cheese."

Behind him, I glimpsed Nicky and Tara floating across the room to the bear costume. "Let's give Colin a little Halloween thrill," Nicky said.

"We don't want to scare him *too* badly," Tara said.

"Of *course* we do," Nicky replied.

I watched Nicky slide into the costume and pull on the mask. Slowly, the bear began to rise from the chair.

I pointed, and Colin spun around.

The bear stood up tall and stretched his big furry forelegs over his head.

"N-no—!" Colin stammered. His eyes nearly bulged out of his head. "It—it's walking! But that's impossible! No!"

The bear stretched its forelegs straight out and came staggering toward Colin.

Colin let out a frightened shriek and tore out of the room. "Mom! Help! Mom! Help me!"

Tara and I laughed as the bear chased Colin down the hall. I ran out to watch. Colin made the stairs, turned, and saw the bear lurching after him.

"Mom! Help me!"

He started down the stairs. Lost his balance and tumbled all the way down. At the bottom, he jumped to his feet and kept running, screaming the whole way.

I heard the back door slam. "He's gone," Tara said. "Did you see the look on his face?"

Nicky came loping back. "I kinda get the idea your brother is afraid of bears," he said.

Laughing together, we returned to my room. The bear costume draped itself over the chair again, and Nicky slid out.

Nicky and Tara are really cool, I thought. I could never get Colin like that on my own.

The phone rang, and I picked it up.

"Hi, Max? This is Traci."

Traci Wayne calling *me*? Was I dreaming?

"Unngh unnngh," I said. I was in total shock.

"Max, I know I said I'd help you with your magic act. But is there any way I can get out of it?"

"Unnngh. Get out of it? Why?" I choked.

"I really don't want to stand that close to you. You're dangerous."

I took a deep breath. Think fast, Max. What can you say to win her over?

"Traci, you won't have to be close to me. I swear."

She groaned. "Okay. What do I have to do?"

"You just have to stand on the trapdoor on the stage. When I raise a curtain in front of you, the trapdoor will go down and you'll disappear. That's all."

"That's all? You promise? And you won't fall on me or drop food on me or embarrass me in front of the whole school?"

"Traci, it'll be a piece of cake. Really. It'll be fun. The trick is totally simple. It'll only take a minute or two. Nothing will go wrong. I promise."

Boy, was I wrong!

22

HALLOWEEN NIGHT. CAN YOU imagine how stressed out I was?

I mean, what if I totally messed up?

What if Joey flew away before I could slide him down my jacket sleeve? What if I dropped the eggs I was juggling and looked like a total klutz in front of two hundred kids? What if the Disappearing Girl trick didn't work, proving to Traci that I am a jerk for life?

Halloween night, and my parents ungrounded me. Mrs. Wright was onstage in the auditorium. All the kids in school were there in their costumes—all except Aaron. He was grounded for Halloween—because he electrified his sister's fairy costume as a surprise and gave her second-degree burns.

It took Mrs. Wright a long time to get the kids quiet. She waved her hands above her head and kept shouting into the microphone. Finally, everyone calmed down.

"We have a special surprise," Mrs. Wright said.

The loudspeakers squealed. She backed away from the mike. "Give it up for some Halloween magic from the Great Max!"

My big moment. I took a deep breath and pushed my cart of tricks onto the stage. Some kids clapped, some booed and hissed—just to be funny.

Someone heaved a rubber bat toward the stage. It hit a kid in the front row in the back of the head. He picked it up and heaved it onto the auditorium balcony. That got a really big cheer.

I signaled the guy in the audio booth, and my music started up. It was a hip-hop beat with lots of scratching. A good rhythm for juggling.

"Here's how I'd like to start out my egg-citing egg-stravaganza!" I shouted. I picked up four hard-boiled eggs from the tabletop, stepped to the edge of the stage, waited for the beat, and started juggling.

The audience grew quiet as I did my two-in-the-air-at-all-times move. But then a boy in the back row shouted, "Max—did you lay those eggs?"

Kids burst out laughing, and I lost my rhythm. Two eggs landed at my feet with a loud *craaaack.* One egg bounced off my knee and into the front row. I held on to the other egg.

Kids were booing and laughing.

Easy, Max, I told myself. Remember the number one magician's rule: Don't panic.

"I meant to do that!" I shouted. "And now, for

my best juggling trick . . ." I began tossing the egg from hand to hand. "One-egg juggling!"

Some kids thought that was funny. Someone tossed a plastic jack-o'-lantern onto the stage. I put the egg down and did some of my easy tricks. I pulled an endless string of handkerchiefs from my coat sleeve. Then I produced a bouquet of flowers from my magic wand.

That went over pretty well. Kids applauded. "Go, Max!" a girl shouted.

"Yeah. Go home!" someone else shouted.

I ignored the laughter and lifted Joey from my upside-down top hat. That quieted them down a little. I held up the pigeon and announced, "I will now make this bird disappear in front of your eyes!"

I held Joey higher and prepared to let him slide down my wide coat sleeve. But he jumped out of my hands and hopped onto the stage.

"Great trick! Do it again!" that same boy in the back row shouted. Ha, ha. Big joke.

I bent down to pick Joey up. But he hopped out of my reach. I stepped forward, grabbed for him again. And again, Joey took two hops away from me.

The whole auditorium erupted in laughter. I could feel my face turning bright red. I made another grab for the stupid pigeon. Missed.

I was ruined, I knew.

My life was over.

I could see Traci at the side of the stage, laughing at me and shaking her head.

"Your act is bombing," a voice beside me said. Nicky!

"No biggie. We'll help you out," Tara said. She swooped down and picked up Joey. She held him in the air and slowly moved him across the stage.

The kids grew very quiet now. How could a pigeon float like that without moving its wings?

I waved my arms toward the bird to make it look like I was making him fly.

I glanced back and saw Nicky pick up the two eggs from the floor. He held them up and made them float too.

Silence in the auditorium. I think they were all amazed by what they were seeing. A floating pigeon and two floating eggs?

"Now for our best trick," Tara said, setting Joey down.

She and Nicky grabbed me around the waist—and lifted me off the floor.

Kids gasped as I floated up and hung six inches off the ground.

"Wow. You weigh a ton!" Tara groaned.

Nicky grasped me under the arms. Tara had my waist. I stretched my arms straight out, and they made it look as if I was flying across the stage—like Superman.

The auditorium was silent for a moment. Then the kids went nuts, cheering and screaming.

"He can fly!" I heard Mrs. Wright exclaim.

"Max, what planet are you from?" a kid screamed from the audience.

"Weirdo! Weirdo! Weirdo!" Someone started the chant, and the whole audience picked it up.

"Weirdo! Weirdo! Weirdo!"

"Put me down—!" I whispered.

"Don't fight us," Tara said. "We're doing you a favor."

"You'll be famous after this," Nicky said.

The two ghosts turned me around and made me fly to the other side of the stage. Traci was standing there at the edge of the curtain, her hands over her mouth. "You're *bizarre*!" she cried. "You're some kind of alien! I'm outta here!" She turned and ran backstage.

"But, Traci—our trick—" I called.

Nicky and Tara turned me, made me spin high in the air, then flew me across the stage again.

"Stop!" I pleaded. "You're scaring me!"

Kids were on their feet, cheering.

Halfway across the stage, Tara cried, "You're too heavy. I can't hold you anymore!" She dropped me. I fell hard, landed on my face and my stomach. I actually said, "Oooof!" which I thought only happened in comic books.

I couldn't breathe for a moment. I guess I had

the wind knocked out of me. I think I heard Nicky say to Tara, "We'd better go." But my head was spinning and the stage tilted up and down under me, so I didn't really know what was going on.

I only knew that while I was sprawled on the stage, I saw a fat brown cockroach crawl out from under the curtain. The cockroach slithered quickly toward me, its antennae straight up. And as it moved, it began to grow.

I watched the insect plump up until it was the size of a chipmunk. *A cockroach as big as a chipmunk!* And now it didn't crawl—it waddled!

I watched it inflate until it grew as big as a cocker spaniel! Its antennae stretched as long as my arms, and the armor on its wet brown back crackled as it moved.

The kids in the auditorium had stopped cheering. As the cockroach inflated, they screamed and shrieked—and stampeded to the exits.

In front of me, the cockroach let out a loud burp. It stretched even bigger, almost as tall as me now, and I could see its gaping mouth, filled with a thick glob of yellow saliva.

I knew what was happening. I knew Phears was about to pay another visit.

And at that moment, my memory snapped back. I suddenly remembered Phears' first visit—Buster turned inside out. It all came back in a horrifying rush. Gasping, I struggled to my feet—in time to see the black cloud rise up from the enormous insect.

Kids were still screaming in horror and running for the doors. I saw Mrs. Wright at the side of the stage, gulping in fright. She turned and ran.

And I was all alone . . . all alone as Phears floated over me.

"Don't move, Max!" he boomed. "Stay right there. My cockroach is very hungry."

23

"NO—PLEASE!" I BEGGED. I raised both hands in front of me as if to shield myself. "Don't let that thing eat me. I already helped you once. Just let me go home."

"But you're not going home—ever again!" Phears shouted. His voice echoed off the walls of the empty auditorium.

Behind him, the cockroach hacked up a disgusting slimeball. Its antennae quivered. Then the insect lowered a spiny tongue and lapped up what it had just coughed out.

"You didn't help me," Phears snapped. "I didn't get Nicky and Tara—did I! They went invisible. So now you're going to help me again. Where are they? They're here with you now, aren't they, Max. Make them appear. Do it—now!"

In the gray mist that swirled around him, I suddenly could see his eyes. Solid white eyes, white as snow, staring coldly.

And I realized Phears wasn't staring at me. He had lowered his gaze to my hand.

"You're wearing the wishing ring, Max," he said, floating closer inside his dark cloud. "That proves you're hiding Nicky and Tara from me."

My throat tightened. I couldn't breathe. Panic swept over my body. I glanced around frantically. "Nicky? Tara? Are you here?" I whispered. "Help me!"

No reply. Where did they go?

"Nicky? Tara?"

A shadowy hand reached out from the fog. "I'll take the ring, Max. It will help me capture your two ghost friends. You won't be needing it—since you'll be slowly, slowly dissolving inside the roach's stomach."

The giant cockroach burped again. Its fat black legs danced on the stage floor as if it was eager to start eating.

Phears' hand grabbed for the glowing red ring.

I jerked it away from him.

Wishing ring? Did he say *wishing ring*?

Did it grant wishes? Could I wish Phears away?

I raised the ring close to my face. It glowed brightly, like a Christmas light. I could feel its warmth radiate against my face.

I took a deep breath. I held the ring close.

I shut my eyes. "I wish I was home safe and sound!" I shouted.

Did I get my wish?

24

I OPENED MY EYES. No.

Phears still floated over me.

"Nice try, Max," he said. "But we both wished at the same time."

I gazed at the ring. Its glow was a little dimmer. Our wishes must have canceled each other out.

I took a deep breath and wished again. "I wish Phears would disappear forever!"

"I wish Nicky and Tara's parents were in my grasp!" Phears shouted at the same time.

The red glow of the ring dimmed to purple.

I didn't wait. Holding the ring to my mouth, I tried again.

"I wish for Phears to be trapped inside that giant cockroach!"

"I wish for Max to dissolve inside the cockroach's belly *while he's still alive*!" Phears made a wish too.

Again, we canceled each other out. In a panic, I stared at the ring. Dead. No color at all.

Phears tossed back his head and laughed. "It's all used up, Max. Now you are helpless."

Phears motioned to the giant cockroach. Its antennae began to rotate wildly. It bobbed its head as it began to lumber toward me. Its mouth pulled open and again I saw the disgusting blob of yellow saliva that roaches use to dissolve their food.

"Nicky? Tara? Can you help me?" I whispered.

I glanced all around as the cockroach swung its huge armored body toward me. And I saw someone peeking out from the curtain. A girl standing at the control panel at the side of the stage.

Traci!

She came back! Was she worried about me?

The cockroach raised its head and sniffed me. A sickening sour aroma fumed from its open mouth.

I tried to run. But Phears used his powers to hold me in place.

Twisting around, I watched Traci. Her mouth was wide with horror. Her hands were pressed to her face. She stood beside the spotlight switch.

Yes. The spotlight switch.

And I had an idea. A last, desperate idea.

Could I give Phears a surprise? Could I startle him long enough for me to scramble away?

I twisted my body. Waved to Traci. I motioned for her to pull the spotlight switch.

She stared back at me, frozen in horror.

I motioned again. Please, Traci. Please understand. Turn on the spotlight. *Pull the switch!*

No.

She didn't get it.

She stared back at me, hands pressed to her cheeks.

Goodbye, Traci, I thought.

The saliva bubbled in the cockroach's open mouth.

I'm cockroach food, I realized.

That's how I'll end up—cockroach food.

25

I GRITTED MY TEETH and waited for the insect to suck me into its drooling mouth.

And then a flash of bright light forced my eyes shut.

I stumbled backward, away from the giant cockroach.

The light swept over the stage.

I heard Phears let out a shrill scream. I opened my eyes and saw him holding up his hands, struggling to shield himself from the bright circle of white light.

Yes! Traci had come through! She had switched on the spotlight.

I thought maybe the bright light would startle Phears and give me time to escape. I had no idea the light would *hurt* him!

But under the spotlight, the thick fog quickly burned away. Phears stood exposed, his solid white eyes blind with panic.

Unable to escape the light, Phears started to shrink. He shrank until he was the size of a rabbit,

then as small as a mouse. Tinier . . . tinier . . . until he was a speck on the stage floor.

An ant. Phears had shrunk to the size of an ant. And as I stared in amazement, Joey wobbled over. The pigeon dropped its head, snapped open its beak, and swallowed Phears.

Joey stared up at me, head tilted, as if expecting another treat. Then he turned, flapped his wings, and flew out the auditorium window—with Phears inside his belly.

Was Phears gone for good?

The giant cockroach had vanished. I ran to the side of the stage. "Thank you, Traci!" I shouted.

But she had run away again from the terrifying scene. How could I ever explain it to her?

I didn't have time to think about that. I ran out the back door of the auditorium and jogged toward home. I had to tell Tara and Nicky what had happened!

I saw a group of trick-or-treaters parading up a driveway across the street. On the next block, kids in ghost and mummy costumes were comparing the candy in their bags. Normal kids. Having a normal Halloween.

I burst into the house and ran up to the safety of my room. I felt like climbing into bed and pulling the covers up over my head.

But there were Nicky and Tara, sitting cross-legged on the floor, dozens of candy bars spread out between them.

"Where were you?" I screamed. "Where *were* you?"

"Trick-or-treating," Nicky said calmly, holding up a bag full of candy.

"Wow. It's so easy to get a *lot* of candy when you're invisible!" Tara said, chewing on a half-eaten Snickers bar. "We just slip into a house and take handfuls!"

"But—but—but—" I sputtered.

"How did the rest of your act go?" Nicky asked. He had a chocolate smear on his chin.

"Go? It didn't go!" I screamed. "How could you go trick-or-treating when I needed your help?"

Tara shrugged. "Easy. The act was bombing. We couldn't stand to watch you flop like that."

"But—Phears showed up!" I cried. "He's still after you. He tried to feed me to a cockroach. But Traci shined bright light on him and he shrank. Then Joey ate him and—and—"

I had to stop to catch my breath.

Tara shook her head sadly. "He'll be back. We haven't seen the last of him."

Nicky shuddered. "We won't be safe until we find our parents."

Tara finished her candy bar and reached for a box of Junior Mints. "But see, Max? You *can* be brave when you get the chance. That's so totally awesome. I'm proud of you." She slapped me on the back with a chocolatey hand.

"But—but—" I sounded like a motorboat starting up. "But—but—"

Nicky shoved away some candy and motioned for me to sit down beside him. "Aren't you glad we're haunting you?" he asked, smiling. "Doesn't it feel good to be a hero?"

I dropped down between them. "Shut up and pass the Milky Ways," I said.

TO BE CONTINUED.

ABOUT THE AUTHOR

Robert Lawrence Stine's scary stories have made him one of the bestselling children's authors in history. "Kids like to be scared!" he says, and he has proved it by selling more than 300 million books. R.L. teamed up with Parachute Press to create Fear Street, the first and number one bestselling young adult horror series. He then went on to launch Goosebumps, the creepy bestselling series that gave kids chills all over the world and made Goosebumps the number one children's series of all time (*The Guinness Book of Records*).

R.L. Stine lives in Manhattan with his wife, Jane, their son, Matthew, and their dog, Nadine. He says he has never seen a ghost—but he's still looking!

Check out this sneak preview of the second book in R.L. Stine's Mostly Ghostly:

Have You Met My Ghoulfriend?

NICKY AND TARA STILL live in Max's bedroom, and while they've found some clues, they still don't know what happened to their parents. Meanwhile, the evil ghost Phears is still desperate to get his hands on Nicky and Tara, and to pressure Max into turning them over, Phears brings a Berserker Ghoul to inhabit Max's body—and make Max go berserk when he least expects it! But Max, Nicky, and Tara aren't giving in to Phears. They have a few tricks up their sleeves—like one very talkative ghost cat, who's taken up residence inside the tunnel to the ghost world. . . .

I FLEW INTO MAX'S room inside a white moth.

I found a hole in the screen and slid right through. I'm used to slipping through small spaces. When you are an Animal Traveler, you can burrow deep or fly high. You can sail away from your enemies and come swooping back to take them by surprise.

At times, I have made myself tiny enough to ride inside a mosquito. I enjoyed the darting, shooting, jumping ride. I have soared inside broad-winged hawks. And I have crept slowly but steadily inside earthworms.

I love to move because I was kept still and in prison for so long. Captured by the Roland parents, the so-called scientists. My last ghostly breath taken from me. Held in a prison that was neither smoke nor spirit nor mirror nor air.

Phears. Phears.

My name struck terror in all who met me.

Until the Rolands took my breath and made me even *less* than a ghost.

But I escaped. My name is Phears and I had to escape. And I had to help the others float free of their prison. And now we ghosts are out. And I sail through the night inside this fluttering white insect.

Tentacles quivering. The air electric. Because I am so close . . . so close to finding the Rolands and having my revenge.

The two Roland kids—Nicky and Tara—will help me. Once I capture them, the parents will come to their rescuc. And I shall have the parents, too. And then I shall destroy all four of them forever.

These are my thoughts as I sail through the night on this unsteady steed. And, of course, I am not alone. I have brought the jabbering Berserker Ghoul with me. What a jolly fellow he is.

He cannot sit still. He drums his hands and taps his feet and shuffles his legs up and down. A bony thing—with his shiny red top hat, red gloves, and striped jacket—rib bones poking out. What is he dressed for? Halloween? Ha, ha.

He was a normal ghoul once, rising up from his grave, staggering through the night, terrorizing people as a ghoul must do. What made him go berserk?

Was it the time I pushed away the shadows and showed him my face? He screamed for hours after that. I don't think he ever recovered.

And now he cannot keep still. He bobs his head and tugs his ears. And jabbers nonsense without stop.

Just the right fellow to teach this boy Max the difference between master and slave. Once my Berserker friend is inside Max, the boy will find himself out of control—and more terrified than any living creature before him.

I wouldn't want this drooling idiot inside *me*!

After a day or so of this ghoul's company, Max will come to me. "Please, Mr. Phears," he will whimper. "Please ask me to do *anything* for you, and I gladly will."

Ha, ha.

He's sleeping so soundly, burrowed in his bed, covers nestled over his head.

I flutter over his hair—so close I can hear his soft breaths.

Softly, softly.

Yes, go, my Berserker friend. Go do your ghoulish work. Yes, slide out of here, hopping and popping and flapping your gums. And try to stay in one place, will you?

I know you Berserkers like to hop from person to person, too jittery, too jumpy, to stay in one place. But I need you to stay inside Max. Stay long enough for Max to come begging on his knees to me. Then you may go jumping and jabbering on your way.